T0198869

FLIGHT OF THE
GYPSY MOTHER

Richard Cook

Order this book online at www.trafford.com
or email orders@trafford.com

Most Trafford titles are also available at major online book retailers.

Printed in the United States of America.

ISBN: 978-1-4669-9714-1 (sc)
ISBN: 978-1-4669-9713-4 (e)

Trafford rev. 06/10/2013

 www.trafford.com

North America & international
toll-free: 1 888 232 4444 (USA & Canada)
phone: 250 383 6864 ♦ fax: 812 355 4082

Contents

Chapter I Contact 1

Chapter II The Gathering..17

Chapter III The Mission..33

Chapter IV Takeoff!...43

Chapter V Aftershock...61

Chapter VI Debriefing 73

Chapter VII Witnesses 83

Chapter VIII Attack Formation......................................97

Chapter IX Maximum Effort..109

Chapter I

Contact

In unison, Linda and Rick sat up in bed.

"What?

"I didn't say anything. I thought it was you. What did you hear?"

"I don't know. It wasn't so much 'heard' as it was like I thought out loud."

"Yeah, me, too. That's exactly how I would describe it. Do you have any idea what it was?"

"I just can't bring anything up about it."

"I can't either. Weird!"

"Well, it didn't come from outside. BJ didn't bark and you know she doesn't miss a thing."

"All I know is that something woke us up and it is 3 hours until time to get up and now I will be counting them down."

Linda noted the time, 3:05. At 3:09 Rick was snoring.

They had been through some interesting times in their lives, almost all having to do with some kind of unexplained activity. In retrospect, they had agreed that most in someway targeted Rick, usually trying to turn him around.

One time, when Rick was on the road, pressing to get home, he went to sleep driving. He knew better—he knew he should have stopped earlier, but once that stone head was set, no amount of reason could penetrate it. He later recalled two loud shouts calling his name, 'Rick! Rick!' which brought him back to consciousness enough for him to realize that the highway was very rough in this area. He then came to be aware that he was on the left shoulder of the highway going 65 miles per hour! Just as he swerved back onto the highway, there was a bridge abutment that he barely avoided with not a second to spare. One thing that did was to ensure that he would not go to sleep again that night, even after he got home. He wondered about the warning . . . who could it have been . . . . , where had it come from? Since he refused to believe any such nonsense as 'guardian angels' as Linda suggested when he told her about it, he consciously put it aside as a stroke of 'good luck'. Even then, his subconscious retained the mystery of it.

Another time, he had gotten out of a meeting earlier than expected. Two men there had come to the meeting in a private plane and were going to return his way. They invited him to join them as they had room for one more. He figured the different flight durations and thought he could still be there about three hours earlier than with his commercial flight. He called Linda to see if she could meet him earlier and she was very happy to be able to do that since the traffic would be much better at that time. He had not had a chance to tell the guys before she called him back, almost in tears.

"Rick, you just cannot take that earlier flight! I can't explain it, but it is so strong that we can't ignore it. If there's any way you can talk the guys into waiting a while themselves, please do it. I know, they'll think you, or your wife, rather, is a fruitcake, but there's something about that time that is wrong, VERY wrong! I will just plan on meeting you at the regular time, PLEASE!!!"

"Hey, no problem at all. I know your premonitions well enough to honor them. I'll just thank them and bow out, and, if given the opportunity, I will see if I can convince them to wait, but from what I have gathered, they came by private plane because of something they were scheduled for earlier than the commercial flight could get them back."

I'm sorry, but it is so strong!"

"Well, don't be sorry. You haven't missed yet, so I am with you whatever you say on this! I will see you later then, and, as they say, better late than never."

Later that evening they were to see on the news about the plane Rick was to get a 'hop' on, having a mid-air collision with another aircraft about 20 minutes after leaving, killing the three on board the private plane. This time, it took a lot more effort to relegate this to another run of 'good luck'. Subconsciously another seed was planted and this time started to grow.

Linda was the spiritual leader in the family. She patiently bided her time, never preaching, just practicing, leading by example, the only real way. Her faith was obviously shining to all who knew her, so it was with some measure of surprise that others noted Rick taking so long to gather enough 'lightening strikes' to finally see the Light. Linda readily admitted that he was her most formidable challenge and through this proved that nothing was impossible for God.

Rick had a good heart, but had that 'God-sized hole' in it, as do all non-believers. And, as is the usual case, all who try to fill that hole with earthly things which never fit, continue to get more frustrated. There was always that need yet to be met so he was never happy with what he had or what he had done. In the process, he very nearly lost his only true treasure on earth, Linda and the kids. They all tried but he was so far gone that he would not listen to anyone, maintaining that there was nothing wrong with him and they should stop trying to make a big thing out of that 'nothing'. 'Nothing', indeed!

The most damaging effects of his actions and attitude were the hurt inflicted on those who loved and trusted him, as well as the destruction of his self-worth by continuing to deny the problem. Nothing? . . . . It was everything! Finally, God, in His Infinite Mercy on Linda allowed Rick to choose himself into a situation where he could not avoid completely evaluating who he was and what was important to him. It was an absolutely life-changing and life saving event when he finally realized that all he ever needed to satisfy that previously unattainable peace within himself was what Linda herself had and what she tried to share with him all this time—Jesus Christ!

With this awakening which brought light to all the dark parts of his heart, Rick was almost overwhelmed with the need to make amends to those whom he had hurt and betrayed. He was very anxious to show everyone what a change in any life, even his, could be affected by allowing Jesus Christ to come in and shine through.

He felt guilty about asking those he had let down so badly for forgiveness, but he understood it to be right to give them the opportunity to forgive him as he had learned in the Lord's Prayer that everyone is told that our Heavenly Father forgives each of us AS we forgive others. When he did see the truth, he couldn't get enough. He felt like he had wasted so much time being miserable about himself that he was trying to catch up. He wanted to see, hear, and most of all, experience God's Works! He often prayed that God would talk to him as He had David or Moses. When he didn't hear, he thought surely his previous sins were too severe and many. Linda assured him that Jesus had already paid for all his sins, past, present and future. She also told him that he was listening too hard and could miss that 'still, small voice'.

"The most effective way to hear and see God is to listen and watch with your heart, not eyes and ears only"

With that aspect of their lives now on track, life in general was much calmer.

When the alarm went off at 6 am, Linda was already up and the morning coffee was brewing. In a few minutes, Rick came in mumbling something about his beauty sleep being disturbed. Linda told him it wasn't doing all that much good anyway. He cut a quick glance, then laughed, telling her it might be a whole lot worse without it.

"Rick, I've been thinking about that 'wake-up' and I can't seem to get it by me. I just cannot remember what it was."

"I know, it's like something that is almost in view, but just can't make it out." After a quiet cup of coffee, trying to recall the mysterious message in the night, they gave up.

"Well, let's get out and hit the road. Maybe the fresh air will help us to remember. Are we getting Alzheimer's? How would we know? If we do get it, let's get it at the same time. Sounds like bliss to me!"

"Don't even joke about something like that!"

On their morning walk, Linda always had her radio with headphones. She liked to walk with her music. Rick always remarked that it was against the laws of physics as well as being geographically impossible that their entire two-mile circuit could be all uphill. Then there was Captain! He was the neighborhood bully, a German shepherd with a penchant for chocolate candy. He would not allow Rick to pass until safe passage was purchased with a piece of candy. 'And I always thought you all were of a noble breed' he would mutter as he paid the ransom.

They had walked for about ten minutes when Linda stopped and held her earphones close to her ears,

"Hon, I just heard it! I just heard what woke me up this morning! It's an ad for Fantasy Flights on the radio."

"That's it! That is what I heard, too! Fantasy Flights . . . what is it?"

"I don't know. That's all I got. As soon as we get back, I'll check the station web page and see what their ads for today are about."

"What could it be? Do you think the radio might have come on for an instant and . . . . nah, that just couldn't be it. It couldn't have just flashed that name and gone off that quickly. The radio was the first thing I checked, after the time. Let's get home and check this out."

After their earlier lives, they were now ready to take it easy and enjoy the Wonders of God's gifts to them; the kids and grandkids and a love that had been truly forged in the furnace of God's Mercy and Grace. They often talked about the spiritual world, angels, demons and the like. Rick was sure that the UFO's were real and he felt equally sure that when God created the heavens and the earth that He very well could have and probably did create other beings in His universe, He also thought that God would limit contact until we could demonstrate a promise of developing a love for others here on earth. Our so-called civilization must be the talk of the universe.

They did agree that there was so much they didn't know about, but also, that understanding wasn't as necessary as the faith they both now had in accepting that it was all under Control. That one thing reinforced his belief that there had been ET presence in so many things on our earth. The pyramids at Giza, the Nasca lines in Peru, the Anasazi star configurations in the desert southwest, so many things world wide we just could not explain away. It satisfied his way of thinking that you believed or you didn't—no halfway measures, no 'cafeteria Christians'. You believe the Bible, then you also believed that our same God created the 'heavens' and the earth. That is all-inclusive and he believed, worth repeating as all was 'under control.'

Coming up the driveway, Rick picked up the paper. Linda went right to the computer and Rick got their coffee. He took Linda hers and went to the den. When he had gotten settled, he opened the paper and a brochure fell right out into his lap. As he picked it up, he yelled,

"Linda, look at this! An insert in the paper for 'Fantasy Flights—Keeping the Past Present'!"

"Well, it's a good thing because there isn't anything on the home page of the station about it."

"Listen to this! They have a B-17, a G model, and we can sign on as crew members for a simulated 'mission', complete with a bombing run and a fighter attack! We have GOT to do this! They have it all! They have a crew breakfast, mission briefing, dawn takeoff, the whole thing! I don't see a cost for it, but whatever it is, I'll find a way! I know, I'll sell my brain to M.I.T."

"Don't you think that it will surely cost more than $1.37?"

"Cute! What do you say? Want to make some history by re-living some history?"

"You know, without trying to figure out what you just said, I am interested in this. For some reason I can't understand, it is important. I guess in light of the message last night, we do need to follow this and see where it goes. You know I'm not much on anything that glorifies war, but this somehow seems different."

"Yeah, I know. To me, this is more like honoring the memory of those who stepped up to do this for all of us. Most everyone agrees that wars are terrible and should only be the last resort, however in this case, there probably is some glorification involved because it was truly a noble cause. They were all aware that this evil had to be met and had really no choice but to fight and to win. It was then their quest. It was being forced on them and they resolved to do their duty and give it their best. That, from the Boeing Company in Seattle, was the B-17 Flying Fortress."

Rick went to the den and got his collection of B-17 data and pictures. For as long as he could remember, he had always been fascinated with the people, places and events of World War II, the air war in Europe and specifically the B-17. It was aptly named, the 'Flying Fortress'. It had ten guns covering all approaches to it, later, more than that. The development of the aircraft was equally impressive.

"Listen to this, 'Responding to the Army Air Corps request for a large, multi-engine bomber, the prototype had gone from the design phase to flight test in less than 12 months! Can you imagine getting that done in today's bureaucracy bog? 'The G model prototype first flew July 28, 1935. It was the first production Boeing military aircraft with a flight deck instead of open cockpit. It had a wingspan of 104 feet nine inches and a length of 74 feet 9 inches. With its gross weight of 65,000 lbs, it had a range of 3,750 miles a ceiling of 35,600 feet and cruised at 150 miles per hour. Boeing built 6,981 B-17s and another 5,745 were built under contract by Douglas and Lockheed. The entire project was a monument to American engineering and ingenuity. The B-17 had a unique and enormous tail section that was necessary for improved control and stability at high altitude bombing. It was the result of such an airworthy design that more than a few returning crew members agreed that they would have not gotten back in a lesser aircraft.' Thought I would just save you some time and read it to you."

"Really, hon, I am interested and I do appreciate your wanting me to be, but I am still mystified by my interest."

Rick was so happy that Linda had taken to this. "When you get a chance, come and look at some of this other stuff. Since you're going to be a crew member, come get to know the beauty you'll be flying in." Rick cheered inside. This was indeed a dream of a lifetime coming true for him, his 'Fantasy Flight' with his soul mate there, too. More blessings than anyone deserved.

He felt he was born a little too late anyway. His favorite music was always the 'big band' sounds, Glenn Miller, Benny Goodman, Artie Shaw and all. As a kid, during the war, it was understood that when you became of age you would join and serve. Many joined before they were 'of age'. Each had their favorite branch of the military and that would be their goal for the war effort. Rick was going to be on a B-17, as his uncle was.

Well, the war ended in 1945 when Rick was 8 years old. By the time he did enter the Air Force, they still had Boeing aircraft, but now the bomber fleet consisted of the sleek B-47 and the big, lumbering B-52, the Stratofortress, what the B-17 had grown into! Both of these bombers were very functional and more lethal than anyone could imagine. They were sterile, highly efficient killing machines, very impersonal, more like doing the business of war rather than the old valor and honor of warriors.

They put the old workhorse of that Great War out to such demeaning pastures as hauling pipe and other cargo, and even used them as targets for the new missiles under development, so far beneath the dignity of a celebrated veteran of so many critical battles. So, with much enthusiasm, Rick was seeing his hero in at least a glow of her former glory. He could hardly believe that he would have a chance to be on a crew and fly a simulated mission on this, the greatest war bird.

Linda had always been a white-knuckled flier, but to her credit, as she met every challenge, she kept at it until she finally was able to enjoy it. That ability was attributed to her unwavering faith which was also instrumental in Rick being able to recognize the power that would turn his life around. Still, she was a bit surprised at the feeling she had about this flight. It's just not something she would normally notice, much less give it a second thought. This was different. She felt a push to accept it but more like a comfortable, natural insistence. She had long since practiced that when something like this arose, she would take it to Jesus. If, after that, she was still at ease with it, she took it as 'approved'.

The brochure instructed that interested parties should call between 0800 and 1700 hours. At 0801, Rick had the number ringing. He had a momentary flashback to his former self when an answer machine picked up, 'Welcome to Fantasy Flights. We keep the past present. Please leave your number and we will call you back within the hour. Thank you for your interest.' This was not what Rick wanted to hear! He was already sold on what the brochure had offered and was ready to sign up! He then realized that this was just a reminder of the 'old self' he so gratefully left behind. There should be no impatience in the Lord as He is always right on time. As he felt the peace of that reminder, he reaffirmed how much more he liked his new self. He left name and number and got some coffee and began to overcome his anxiety during his wait.

"Angel, what do you think of all this? I know we've been through some weird things, but this is shaping up to be a new indoor record!"

"Well, as I have said, I am strangely interested. I expected you to be all over this, but I just can't explain how I feel. I was thinking about Tom and Karen, having lived through those dark times as kids in Germany. Remember them telling us about the raids, the British during the night and the Americans during the day? I just can't begin to imagine living through that. Bad as it was, they were blessed to live through it. The damage to those centuries-old cities, the fire storm at Dresden, it all is such a terrible waste."

"Yeah, everybody loses in a war. The British had a rough go of it themselves with the bombings and the V-1 and V-2 rockets. Hitler was determined to bomb them into submission. Just think how it must have been to try to carry on living, never knowing what would hit next or where. I think the guys that went to England from here had no problem getting motivated to do what they could to stop that madness. Seeing the effects first hand, on both sides, it didn't take much imagination to translate that damage and suffering to their own cities here at home. They knew it had to be stopped there."

"Rick, what do you think would have happened if England had fallen?"

"That question has been debated since the war, and nobody knows for sure, but it would have been extremely more difficult without England as a base of operations for the bombers. The war could have been extended possibly long enough to allow Germany to develop the atomic bomb. They were uncomfortably close as it was. Had that come about, with their rocket program, the outcome could have been much different. One article I read talked about the problem with Hitler's madness holding back progress of weapon systems they had developed. They had a ground-to-air missile which carried 660 pounds of high explosives along a directional beam to 50,000 feet and with great accuracy. It could have wiped out allied air power over Germany had Hitler allowed the switch from the V-2 program to that system. Several other highly effective technical developments were not pushed that could have significantly changed things, such as the Heinkel HE 210 Owl, a night fighter, most advanced, and of course, the jet ME 262 Stormbird and the rocket plane, ME 263 Komet. General Adolph Galland of the Luftwaffe high command was on record saying with 200 to 300 ME 262's, the American offensive could have been stopped in one week. Now, aren't you glad you asked? It is a good question to ponder. The debate continues. I'm just glad we didn't have to find out. I guess of all the critical points in human history, the battle for Britain has to rank way up there. It was truly God's Providence that guided that effort and, of course, He used my B-17's!"

When the phone rang, Mr. 'calm and patient' almost dropped it. It was Abel MacLelland from Fantasy Flights. Mac, as he asked to be called, briefly went over the brochure information and asked that, if still interested, they come to the Exeter Inn on Thursday evening for dinner and a detailed presentation. Naturally, Rick agreed and both were put on the roster. When he hung up, he realized that,

"Hey, tomorrow is Thursday! Kinda short notice, isn't it?" Linda asked if he knew any reason they couldn't make it. "Well, uh, no, not really."

"Besides, you would be a basket case if we had to wait a few days."

"You're right about that!"

"Rick, something is up with this whole thing. I can feel it and it is so powerful—not scary, just awesome."

"Yeah, I've been having a running battle with my imagination and can hardly wait to see what comes next, but I do have that same strong feeling that there is something really beyond what we can even consider right now."

He called Phil, a good friend and neighbor, to see if he might know something about 'Fantasy Flights'. Phil had not heard of it, but said he would see if Edith, his wife, had seen anything about it or noticed a brochure in the paper.

"Surely Sam knows about this. Let's call them." Any excuse to call the kids. Sure enough, Sam had seen one of the Fantasy group at an air show. He thought it sounded great and urged them to do it, as if Rick needed any encouragement! He, too, thought it sounded a bit eerie when they told him about the events leading up to the day. In a few minutes, Phil came by. Rick showed him the brochure.

"Well, it does look like fun and something you would really be up for. I have talked to some in the neighborhood and nobody received that brochure, and we all subscribe to the same paper. "Nobody heard anything strange last night or heard anything on the radio or TV about Fantasy Flights?"

"Not a soul."

"Angel, this is going to be one of those things!"

"It's obvious to me that you two have been chosen for something special. You can bet we will be waiting, not patiently, I might add, to hear the details as they come about. We will pray for your guidance and protection in whatever this turns to."

"Thank you, old friend and we do appreciate that. I can't help but get excited about the promise this seems to be headed toward."

"You know, I recall you telling me that you were always asking God to talk to you. Well, I would tell you to remember the saying, 'be careful what you ask for', but we all feel nothing but positive about this, so just hang on and enjoy the ride."

It was a fitful night of dozing on and off for Rick. He just couldn't leave it alone. Linda was sleeping peacefully, but as was his nature, he was again trying to analyze all of this. That is, until he finally remembered that he was falling into the old enemy trap, his one-of-hundreds of favorite sayings was 'worry is a result of the lack of faith'. Amazing! The devil never quits! He immediately focused on the blessings God was sending him and how exciting it would be for him and Linda and quickly dropped off to a deep, restful sleep.

The next morning, both awoke fresh and rested. When they had their morning prayers and got their coffee, they both remarked as to how quiet they were.

"You know, I think maybe we are a bit apprehensive as to what this day may hold for us. Not bad, mind you, just that unknown factor."

"Yeah, I agree. I see it as more anticipation, like wondering about that special package under the Christmas tree and what it could be."

"Good analogy! Well, let's get on our two-mile climb! You listen for any more messages and I will try to take care of the four-legged mugger on the corner."

As they got out into the cool morning air, the day just seemed to be more alive than usual. The sky was clean, the air more crisp, the flowers and greenery were all more definite.

"Rick, I think this is what God wants us to see every day. This is what living life is all about—appreciating all He has created for us to enjoy".

"We better get ready for the heist! We're getting close to Mrs. Johnson's house. That is her name, right?"

"Yes, at least that's what I heard. I've got to do something about this. I feel too guilty about her. I never see her out but we've just got to stop by and visit with her and get to know her."

"So far, no Captain. 'Captain', huh! Probably for Captain Blackbeard!"

By this time, he usually came charging out, barking with that fake menacing curl of his lips being belied by his wagging tail.

"Ha! She hasn't let him out yet! We got a break today. Want some candy?"

Then they heard him barking inside the house.

"Sorry fella, you missed out today."

As they got closer to the house, his barking became more frantic. They could see him running from one window to the next, barking to them, not at them.

"Rick, maybe we better see . . ."

He was already heading toward the door.

"Something is wrong, for sure."

He got to the door and tried it. He found, to his relief, it was not locked. He knocked once and Captain was all over the door, inside whimpering. When Rick opened the door, Captain met them. He wheeled around and ran to the kitchen and back to them, barking all the while.

Linda called to her and heard a weak response. They ran into the kitchen and found her lying on the floor, Captain licking her face. She was barely conscious, but was able to talk to Linda, who was checking her out while Rick called 911. When the ambulance was on the way, he came back into the kitchen. "Rick, she is diabetic—her sugar got too low and she passed out and fell, she thinks she broke her hip. She can't move."

"Hi, Mrs. Johnson, I'm Rick. The ambulance is on the way." Linda had given her a piece of candy that was on the table. She had been trying to get to it when she went out.

After a bit she came more out of the stupor and tried to sit up "Feeling a little better now?"

"I think so, but my hip sure seems to be broken. It hurts a lot and I can't move my feet."

"They will be here shortly and then get you taken care of." "Thank God you all were close by and heard Captain. I see you two walking by here just about every morning but I just never got a chance to say 'hi' to you."

"Well, we both apologize for that and can assure you that changes right now. You are hereby part of our walk routine every day! We were surprised that Captain wasn't out to meet us today. He and Rick have this game going—he 'threatens' to not let Rick pass until Rick pays him off with a piece of candy." "Captain!!! Shame on you!"

"Linda, look at that. I swear he is blushing!"

"He acted as if he sensed something was wrong with me today. I like to have never gotten him to go outside this morning and when he did, it was only for a short time then he was asking to be let back in. He wouldn't let me out of his sight. I knew I had gotten myself in low-sugar trouble, you can always tell, and waited a little too long to try to get a quick lift with the candy. When I came around, Captain was licking my face and barking right at me, but I just couldn't move. So, I don't know what would have happened if you two hadn't come along. I would have surely gone out again and more than likely, not come out of that one. So, again, thank God for you."

When the EMT's were checking Mrs. Johnson, Rick got Captain away from her by talking to him and petting him, speaking to him as if he were another person. He licked Rick's hand as if to say 'thanks'. Rick opened the candy bar and offered it to Captain and he was so thankful that Linda was there to witness Captain putting his nose under Rick's hand and pushing it back toward Rick. He was tearfully moved by this gesture. He broke it in half and only after Rick had eaten his half did Captain eat the one Rick had given him.

"Mrs. Johnson, we'll take care of Captain, so don't worry about him."

"Oh, thank you so much. His food is there in the kitchen and you can go through the back yard and back door. I won't lock that. He has a door he can go in and out when he needs, so thank you so much again. I know God has truly blessed me this day by sending you to me."

"I just hope she is okay through this. Rick, she is 88! I'm thinking now that this is about us not getting too self-centered to watch for needs in others right here under our noses that would be our responsibility, such as Mrs. Johnson. There is no reason for us not taking a few minutes even just once in a while to stop by and see how she was doing. I feel so badly about that."

"You know I feel the same way, but, as you told her, we correct that today! I still can't get over Captain acting that way. It was the most sincere 'thank you' I have ever seen. I take back all the complaints I ever thought about him."

Chapter II

The Gathering

They got back on the road with a different appreciation of the day.

"Something like that does bring your senses to bear. I feel like I can hear the grass growing. Just thought everything was fine-tuned this morning earlier! No question, we were directed to the right place and time and it is such a good feeling. I repeat what I said earlier, this is how I think God wants us to live every day!"

Later that afternoon, Linda called the hospital and was put right through to Mrs. Johnson's room "Hi, this is Linda. How are you doing? . . . . Mrs. Johnson, that is wonderful news . . . . yes ma'am, Martha it is then . . . . well, how long do they plan to keep you? . . . . Oh really! . . . . That is great! . . . . Yes ma'am, Captain is fine. He misses you but he is taking his job of watching over things very seriously. I think the place is in good hands. We went down a bit ago and made sure he had water and he was happy to see us. We will check on him often, so you just take it easy, enjoy the rest and we will see you later. Yes ma'am, we will check back with you tomorrow . . . . good night."

"Her hip wasn't broken, thank the Lord for that! It was like a stinger, I guess. She already has full movement so they will probably keep her tonight and let her come home tomorrow or Saturday maybe. I dreaded the worst for her if that hip was broken. I don't think she has any family."

"Well, she has us!"

"She does and I thank God for the opportunity to maybe make amends for not getting to know her sooner."

They called Phil and Edith and brought them up to date on her status. They insisted they be involved in helping where they could. Rick told them to come over and they would all go down and let them meet Captain and get to know where things were.

They all gathered and walked to the old but warm house on the corner. It had been there as long as anybody could recall. It was there when they all had built their houses, but it never looked run-down or in any kind of disrepair. A couple of the neighborhood kids kept the lawn trimmed and mowed, but Mrs. Johnson was rarely seen outside. She would later confess that she didn't want anybody to 'make a fuss over her' because of her age and wanted to remain independent as long as possible, which they could all understand. However, that didn't help to relieve their guilt for neglecting a visit to her sooner.

"Can you believe she takes such good care of this place? I wonder if she would come clean our house! She could probably give us all some pointers on how to do it right!"

When they came through the back yard, Captain was right there to meet them. Rick went in, followed by Linda and they had to endure the jumping and barking of his greeting.

"Captain, this is Phil and Edith, our friends and now your friends. They will be here to visit and check on you and your mother when she comes home."

He looked quizzically at them, with his ears up and head cocked, then made a low whimper. Phil and Edith both put their hands out and he licked one then the other, then the tail wagging began. "I think you are IN"

They both petted him and told him they were glad to meet him. They were indeed 'in' as he now had their scent, taste and sound of their voices. He ran over to where his food was kept, which they noted was certainly within his reach, but he had not touched the bag. They fed him and made sure his huge water bowl was full and fresh, then all walked outside with him to let him get some outside air.

"This is a unique one."

"He sure is to us." They related the events of the morning,

"He knew we would be coming by and he was waiting for us. I don't know how deep his reason goes, but, here again, he is one of God's creatures and God gives him what he needs when he needs it."

"I think if we hadn't come up to the house and had just kept walking, he would have come through one of those low windows there in the front room. He knew she needed help and soon, so we were it"

"I tell you, something powerful is going on. You two are right in the middle of it and now I, WE feel we are in it too!"

"Well, welcome and we couldn't have better company on this adventure."

On their way back to Rick and Linda's, they were seeing each house in the neighborhood in a different light. Who lives there? Any special needs?

"We've got to have a block party."

"Sounds great to me"

"Right. When Mrs. Johnson gets home, we're doing just that! My goal is to have everybody, except Mrs. Johnson, on a first-name basis and live here like the Lord wants to."

"That sounds like a worthy goal and count us in on that, too." "This just emphasizes what we thought earlier about being shown how God expects us to act and live. It's funny how we can read the Word, memorize it even, but if we don't put it into practice, we haven't done anything worthwhile!"

"So right, my friend. We'll call Mrs. Johnson this evening and introduce ourselves. What's that saying? 'It's never too late to make amends and it's always your turn!"

"I like that! Truly words to live by."

Linda immediately went in and got on the computer. She typed a note as follows:

> Do you know your neighbor, your others?
>
> The same ones that live on your street?
>
> They are all our sisters and brothers
>
> So, if not, it's past time to meet.
>
> God put us here for His Plan,
>
> To comfort our neighbor in need,
>
> But if we never know them from Dan,
>
> How can we hope to succeed?

Get to know those around you! There's no telling what blessings you are missing!'

She then sent it to all the kids, then to everyone on her e-mail list. God wasn't going to have to tell her twice!

The time finally came to go to the Exeter Inn. Naturally, they were early, unable to restrain Rick any longer. Walking up to the entrance, they noticed a couple behind them with one of the brochures from 'Fantasy Flights'. Rick introduced Linda and himself, explaining that they too were going to the briefing. The couple, Bob and Sue Foster, sounded as anxious as Rick and Linda about this program.

"Did you all experience anything unusual associated with this thing?"

"Matter of fact, we did! We heard something earlier in the night that we couldn't recall until Linda heard it later on the radio. When she heard 'Fantasy Flights', she and I both recalled that is what we heard."

"That's exactly what happened to us, except we heard a flash, just a spot ad on TV about it and that's when we remembered it!" "And the brochure, we seem to be the only ones on the block that have received it in our paper."

"Same with us! What in the world is going on with this?"

"Well, we're hopefully about to find out . . . here we are."

They were directed to one of the Inn's meeting rooms where they found two other couples already there.

"And I thought we were early!"

After introductions all around, Bob then asked the others about any unusual experiences with this. They all had gotten the wake-up call at the same time and couldn't remember what it was until they heard it later again, one on the radio and one on TV. And, to make it unanimous, they, too, were the only ones on their blocks to receive the brochure! That caused a moment of silence but only a moment. They all seemed to be of one mind on this and were anxious to see more.

As they talked, they also found that they all were about the same age, from varied backgrounds, but had a common interest in that same era for one reason or another, had family, either father or uncle who had flown in B-17's during the war and all had a deep, abiding faith in God.

Then Able MacLelland came in. He introduced himself as the pilot and asked to please be called Mac. He introduced Charles Moore, his co-pilot, who asked to be called Chuck. As he greeted each one, he gave them a schedule of events for the flight. Meanwhile, Chuck was setting up the display showing pictures of the B-17, the interior, past 'crew' photos and, of course, hats and T-shirts for sale. Mac was speaking,

"I have heard some of the happenings that you had experienced and wanted to let you know that this flight was unusual from my standpoint in that all flights before and the two already scheduled after this one were all overflows with waiting lists. This one had generated only four calls, the four couples now present. I don't know what the difference may be, the area, time of year or what, but we do have a full complement if you are still 'go'!"

Of course, that generated a repeat discussion about the ads in the paper and on the radio and TV, about two hearing the ad on the radio and the others on TV, the brochures and all having the 'wake-up' message at the same time!

Mac was more than a little mystified and told them they had only used the flyers in the paper and had put nothing on radio or TV about it. The flyers were always sufficient supplement to the web site for any ads they needed for a flight in a particular area. "And we always need to schedule additional flights in each area. This one is unique"

"Then there is no reason that you would need a gimmick or mystery ad to promote your flights."

"Absolutely none, Rick. I don't understand what you people witnessed, but I can assure you we didn't initiate any audio or video ads."

Rick added that, as best they could determine, the four couples there were the only ones to receive the brochures as well. Linda spoke up to break the silence,

"As if it mattered! You would go if the Red Baron himself appeared and told you about this!"

"Especially!"

Mac was getting more comfortable now that the 'crew' was set and committed. This would be a good group, strange circumstances and all. He said,

"You all are adding new meanings to our name, 'Fantasy Flights!'"

They all laughed, feeling they were coming more together in this and couldn't wait to go. This was going to be something much more than they had even dreamed of when they decided to call about it.

It was a special group. Bob and Sue Foster were both family of veterans who had served on B-17's during the war. Bob's father was a pilot and Sue's uncle was a bombardier. Ken and Marianne Wilson also were 'doubles'. Ken's uncle was a ball turret gunner and Marianne's father was a radio operator. Allen Collier's father was a tail gunner and his wife Charlotte might as well have been there herself. A pilot, she just couldn't get enough of learning of and trying to experience the events of that era and the B-17's role in it. They all wanted to revive the memories of those they knew as well as those they didn't who had been a part of this exciting and critical time in our history.

They all ordered dinner and the conversation sounded like a high school reunion! They had bonded immediately and rattled on like old friends. After dinner, Mac went to the podium and again formally welcomed them.

"Our main goal in doing this is not to make a bunch of money. We, of course want to make expenses and make our time worth while, but, believe it or not, our passion is preserving the memory of what those before us did with this airplane. We all, from our CEO to every member of our ground crew, love our jobs. Our objective is to relate that passion to youall by trying to include you in a time of such importance that we won't let it pass into oblivion."

"We will meet at the old Foster Army Air Corps field, Bob, any family ties here?"

Bob said he was proud to say that there was; it had been named after his grandfather, who served in World War I.

"Those of you who aren't familiar with it, it is about six miles north of town on highway 1108. We chose that site as it more closely resembles the fields our B-17's are 'comfortable with."

Rick and Linda lived south so they were about an hour from the field. Everybody else lived close to it. Mac continued,

"We will gather at the field at 0500 for an authentic G.I. breakfast in the hangar there, then have our mission briefing, initial station assignments, then our walk-around inspection of our aircraft. We will take crew photos with the plane, then board for a sunrise take-off. Our mission will consist of a bombing run on a target in the old Foster Field bombing range. We have four 'bombs', sandbags filled with different colored sand. The pair to drop their bomb closest to the target bulls-eye will take home a special prize. Since we will be doing an actual drop, we will be taking special precautions with you using safety harnesses in the bomb bay area. The bomb bay doors will open and the 'bomb' will drop on your command and we have, by the way a real Norden bombsight."

Rick was about to bounce off the wall.

"Coming off the target, be especially alert for a beautifully restored Messerschmidt 109 attacking us. You gunners will have lasers mounted on your guns, which are completely plugged, by the way, so when you score a 'hit' on the 109, it will start smoking. So, it's up to you to save our hides! Any questions so far?"

Rick, of course,

"Yeah, can we go right now?"

Everybody chimed in on that.

"We will rotate you through all the stations, so you can at least have an idea of how it all works. And, of course, we will go over all the details in the mission briefing on Saturday morning. The weather forecast is CAVU for the weekend so everything looks great."

Marianne asked about CAVU.

"I'm sorry Marianne, that stands for Ceiling And Visibility Unlimited, perfect flying weather. The way this flight is shaping up, I'm not at all surprised at that forecast."

"We have here photos of some of our past crews with their aircraft, the interior of them, also pictures of the 'old ladies' during actual combat. There are some other brochures you may take to friends and family, or maybe you would rather wait and see just how bad it is!"

Ken said there wasn't a chance it could be bad from what he had already heard. That thought was unanimous. After much discussion about what Mac had told them, all were anxious to get on with it. This looked to be an event of a lifetime for each of them. Mac had to almost drive them out after he and Chuck had packed the presentation display. He told them again that there was something special in many ways about this flight. They all felt it.

On the way home, Rick and Linda were quite wound up. Linda remarked how she had never seen eight perfect strangers come together so quickly. They were as one, having come from different backgrounds and never meeting before, but after this one evening, they all centered on the amazing Boeing B-17.

"Rick, this gets weirder all the time. Is there any doubt in your mind that all of us were chosen for this flight? I was just trying to figure out how we could have all been brought together, first as couples, then all located in this area, THEN responding to this ad."

"Too much for my $1.37 brain to process. We both know there is no such thing as coincidence but what in the world could something like this have to do with any kind of Divine activity? We've got some serious talking and praying to do or I'll grind on this all night."

"You heard Mac. They have dozens of these flights, all sold out all over the country, so what is special about this one?

"Linda, we have seen all the attention the B-17 gets at the air shows, all the caps, belt buckles and shirts, so why not in this time and place? There is nothing special about anyone in the group, at least that we are aware of, so what is it? It may be that hard as it is to admit, we are the only four couples that are interested and totally sold on God. That is the basis I got from all of us. I don't know what else it could be. Linda, you know that I am sure that nobody is more in tune with the Spirit than you—maybe it is you in the group."

"Well, whatever it is, we can only pray for guidance to carry out His Plan for us. I don't know for sure, but I feel pretty confident that something in this flight is to be used in His Plan, so we just have to wait in His time. We've got all day tomorrow to stew about it, or we can enjoy the anticipation of an experience of a lifetime—I know what the old Rick would do, so, with the new one, I'm looking forward to having a great time thinking about this with you."

"You always know how to get me centered and I thank for it and love you for it, too! Let's look at those pictures some more. Hey! We've got those tapes of "12 O'clock High" and "Memphis Belle" we can watch! Now we can look at them with a new perspective!"

When they got home, Rick found and started one of his most favorite movies, "12 O'clock High" and found to his amazement in his 'valuable stuff drawer' the pocket-sized new testament his uncle had given him. It had the wing and propeller Army Air Corps insignia on it and the foreword was by President Franklin Roosevelt. This he would take along to make one more flight in a plane like it had flown with so many times in the past. He couldn't help but think about Fantasy Flight's slogan, and he felt that he was already making the 'past present and he loved it!

They both watched the movie with particular interest in the flying parts this time, taking note of the placement of the yokes, throttles, gauges, even the tail wheel lock. It was as though they were absorbing these details for some reason other than just their heightened interest. The story line was a distant second this time around.

After the movie ended, it was like they both came back to reality from a trance.

"Rick, I didn't realize that the B-17 had an autopilot. Did you see when Gregory Peck made the slow turn to let the formation catch up, he turned some knob there on the console, or was that the trim tab on the rudder? Rick, where did I get that?"

Rick stared at her for a moment,

"I don't know . . . . but you know how many times I have watched this movie . . . . this time I saw things I never noticed before! This is getting spookier all the time. Linda, you wouldn't have cared about or known a trim tab from a diet drink before tonight."

Long silence . . . . "I know, it was all of a sudden just there. I'm going to bed! Enough of this for tonight." Rick would not sleep much this night. He wanted to talk. He thought of calling one of the 'crew'. All of them had exchanged contact numbers, but he decided it was probably too late. He would just wait until in the morning.

Friday morning—Linda came into the den to find Rick asleep in the chair, the TV still on and "Memphis Belle" still in the VCR. She didn't know how long he had been asleep, so she didn't wake him. She poured some coffee and thought about how the movie they had watched last night had affected her. She couldn't help but feel the impact of, when one of those B-17's went down, that related to 10 men, killed or captured! One raid she recalled reported that 60 planes were lost—that was 600 men. And that was just one instance in the early 40's. She was building a deepening respect for those who were there and an extreme interest in that aircraft and the time. She prayed that God give her the wisdom to recognize and respond to what He wanted her to do with all of this. It was promising to be something that she didn't want to be asleep at the wheel when it came along. Rick smelled the coffee and came in the kitchen,

"Morning angel, guess I finally ran out of adrenalin and went out in the middle of the co-pilot going back to fire the tail gun. I was wondering if that was maybe against SOP to leave one pilot on the flight deck in the middle of an attack. I just thought about the pilot getting hit and him being in the back where one of the crew would have to get up there and try to fly the plane. I carried that thought to sleep because I dreamed I was in the pilot seat and you were the co-pilot! How scary is that!"

"I don't remember hearing Mac describe those stations as ones we will rotate through and, for me, that's fine—I know you would jump at a chance at it, but lets just leave that part to them were they belong."

"You're right, angel. I would love to fly that beauty, but only after some good instruction. I can't imagine getting in there cold and trying it. I think we will have all we can handle at the other stations. I'm anxious to get to that Norden bombsight!"

"Tomorrow, Rick, tomorrow."

"Rick, I've heard all I need to hear about the infamous 'green eggs' in the military, and I don't know what we may have in the morning, but just in case, I'm taking us some breakfast tacos and coffee."

"Hey, that's great with me—I've never been able to say that I liked those powdered eggs. Do we have the bacon, egg and potato ones?"

"Of course—running out of them would be like being out of Alka-seltzer."

Linda called Edith and asked them for dinner to keep Rick from exploding. He would create his 'burnt offering' of chicken on the grill and, with the company, would maybe get through the evening. To say he was anxious was understating the understatement.

Phil and Edith came over as Rick was putting the chicken on the grill.

"Rick, for as long as I have known you, which goes back to our dim history of the first grade, you have always been a pilot at heart, and we've had so many discussions about the air war in Europe, so I know this is such an event for you, especially."

"Yeah, I guess you could say that I have given it a thought or two."

Linda, from the kitchen, faked a laughing cough. Edith told them that from what they had heard, this sounds like a preview of a 'Twilight Zone' episode!

"We have both prayed about it and knowing you both, we never sense anything but positive about this. So, whatever youall are going into, we can't wait to hear the details."

"I've got the video camera ready to go, so we will have a 'review' when we get back. Wish you two were going along."

Rick spoke up, jumping ahead as usual,

"If this is half as exciting as I think it will be, we can all do another one together."

Phil asked if we got to actually fly the plane.

"No, that wasn't one of the rotation stations."

"Just wondered. Last night I dreamed I saw you both in the cockpit, Rick in the left seat, Linda in the right, and seriously flying that plane."

"Funny you should mention that. Well, nothing is actually funny about this whole thing anymore, but Rick dreamed the same thing last night. Fun as that sounds, we both agreed that was maybe a far piece beyond our capabilities."

"It was plain as day—in fact, Linda was, at first, there alone, then you came up and got into the left seat."

"Me flying that thing alone? You had a nightmare! We better make sure they have parachutes for us all."

Everybody had a good laugh about that, but it was still stored as another piece of this strange puzzle.

After dinner, as they were leaving, Phil said,

"You are both in for an adventure, so enjoy it totally. You are always in God's hands, so there is no reason to have the slightest concern."

"Sure, easy for you to say! Seriously, I know you are right. I'd go tonight if they would let us. Oh, hang on for a minute and let me call Mrs. Johnson again."

"That would be good. We need to see what the latest is with her anyway."

"Martha, how are you? This is Linda just checking on you for the latest . . . . Oh really? . . . . well, while you're already there, might as well get it done. I know you are anxious, but Captain is doing fine and we'll check on you later. Take care, now." "Well, the doctor wants to run all the tests on her that he hasn't been able to get her there for before, so will keep her until probably Tuesday now. Can youall check on Captain for us tomorrow?"

"Of course, be glad to."

"Great, then we're set to go!"

"We'll check with Mrs. Johnson early tomorrow and see if she needs us to bring her anything, too, so we've got her taken care of. Just enjoy!"

Chapter III

The Mission

They were to be up at 0330 and loaded and be on the way by 0400. As usual for Rick, whether it be fishing or this, he couldn't sleep for the anticipation, that is, until about 0300 when he got very sleepy. But when the alarm went off at 0330, he was up and on the floor. Linda got up and started the tacos while Rick poured the coffee.

"At last!"

He kept muttering 'this is it!'. Linda smiled seeing the sheer joy of the moment in him that would affect anyone.

When all was ready, they knelt and prayed thanksgiving for the day and the blessings they were sure to receive and for all who would be involved this day. They put on their 'official' A-2 leather jackets, loaded up and got on the road.

It was a cool, clear April morning and the stars were brilliant. This was going to be a great day. Rick's mind was racing with the promise of what was to come. Linda noticed and broke in,

"Rick, for whatever reason, it just came to me that the excitement of this event is another example of how our life should be every day, just like we discussed yesterday morning. Think we are getting a double dose of it to make sure we get it? We do have an eternity ahead of us that we can't begin to imagine how wonderful it will be. Nothing on this earth should be able to dampen that spirit. So, no matter how amazing this day will turn out to be, what we have to look forward to can't even be considered in the same light."

"Now that is a point! You know how I feel right now . . . . I can't imagine feeling this every minute, but you are right, every day should be this full."

As they got on the freeway, they noticed that there was no traffic. Even at this hour, week-end or not, there was always traffic. Linda set the radio on a local news-talk station to see if there was a problem anywhere. So far, no mention of anything that would hold up traffic.

They had gone about 15 miles when, like running through a curtain, they were enveloped in a fog bank thicker than either of them had ever seen. They couldn't see the front of the car!

"Thank God there isn't any traffic! Can you see the shoulder over there?"

"Only if I look straight down."

"Okay, I'm going to ease over as far as I can so let me know."

"Right, come on more, I can see the edge . . . go ahead and get two wheels off the pavement. Okay, that should be good for now."

"I'm leaving the park lights on, of course but will also leave the motor running. I haven't seen fog like this ever, even in England in the 50's! At least there we could see the center stripe, even if it was on the wrong side of the road!"

"What? How can a center stripe be on the wrong side of the road?"

"It was *there*!"

Rick thought how this was the new 'him', remembering that in the past, having something like this holding up a dream of a lifetime, he would have gone completely off, probably at God, for doing this to him. Now, he was concerned as to how this came up so fast and how it might hold the others up, but not in the least for what it was doing to them. He, in fact, told Linda that this was going a bit too far with the 're-creation' of wartime England for their mission.

After about fifteen minutes, they called Mac.

"Mac, this is Rick—we're in the worst fog I have ever seen. We're still about 20 minutes from the field, but we just can't move in this. Youall go on with the breakfast and we'll get there as soon as we can. We've got some coffee and breakfast tacos we brought along just in case, so it's a blessing that we did."

"Okay Rick, we will go on and eat and you just get here when you can do it safely."

"We'll do that and hope to see you shortly."

"No big rush. We'll be here when you get here."

"Thanks, Mac" "It was a good idea to bring those tacos along. Let's have some! Besides, I'm sure they will beat those 'green eggs' anyway."

About 0515 the fog lifted as if it were that same curtain being raised. They immediately got under way.

"Ever see the fog clear like that, with no sun or wind?"

"Why are you surprised?"

They called Mac to let him know they were moving and would be there in 20 minutes barring any other surprised.

Then the airfield came into view as Rick was getting pumped up again. As they turned into the field, the main hangar was straight ahead. They rounded the building and there it was— the "Gypsy Moth er"! Weird name, but she was beautiful. They just stopped and put the sight into their memory banks. This was, for sure, a special lady.

They parked and went in the hangar where the others were in their briefing. Entering the old hangar was another step back in time. The huge structure was built in the 1940's and was certainly large enough to accommodate several of any aircraft of it's day, even three 'Gypsy's!

Off to one side were the offices and a large maintenance cage which had at one time housed everything from bolts and rivets to spare engines. On the other side were two classrooms, now used primarily for ground school classes. With the addition of the new 'sports pilot' license, there was quite a surge in business since there were so many who wanted to fly just to be flying, not for business and could get a restricted license to fly themselves only. It required much less cost of instruction time and the testing was not so rigorous as the private pilot license.

The 'crew' was assembled in the larger of the two classrooms, which had regular school desks and a platform for the instructor Behind him was a pull down screen and off to one side a authentic replica of a target chart with a big red X circled.

"Look at this, Linda. If this was a Quonset hut, I would expect to see Gregory Peck standing up there in a flight suit!"

"It sure is a perfect setting for this program."

Just out the window, in the lights, being made ready was the lady of the hour, 'Gypsy Mother'

Mac stopped and welcomed them, said they hadn't missed much of the briefing and turned again to the target on the screen. Sue Foster whispered they had not missed much when they missed breakfast either. She said it just didn't taste right to her, but she wanted to experience what 'G.I.' food was like and ate it all, as they all had done. She mentioned Mac saying something about the radio, but they had that covered with no problem and was now presenting the target for their bomb runs.

"Today, we have a target that is of the utmost importance. Today, for the first time, we attack the enemy's silicon supply! As you know, without silicon, the enemy landing on the English coast cannot happen as there aren't enough suitable beaches there for an amphibious assault. The enemy's diabolical scheme, we have been informed, is to take the beach with them on the first wave! So, it is up to us to take that option from them and destroy the silicon supply!"

Everyone cheered and applauded.

"We will approach straight in at 3,000 feet. There should be little cross wind so what you see is what you should hit."

Chuck then got up, "Here is the Norden bombsight and you will see the 'pickle switch' here, this releases your bomb. We will have the bomb doors open and set up on approach so all you have to do is, when the crosshairs, here, are on the target, this 'X' here, you press the button on the switch and it's bombs away."

Mac came up again, "As we mentioned, closest one to the center wins a plaque designating you as a master bombardier of the Gypsy crew. Rick and Linda, you are up front to begin as navigator and nose gunner, so you'll lead off. Then, we will rotate stations up from there. Sue and Bob, you'll be next up. It will take a few minutes to come around because we want everything to be the same for everyone and during that time is when you can expect the fighter attacks, so get in your new positions asap and be ready! Remember, the United Kingdom is counting on you!"

"Again, this should be a great trip and we want it to be all you expect and more. We don't have a jeep to take us to our plane, but, since it is just outside, I think we can all make it. We will do our crew photos then do our walk-around to make sure we have all the parts needed to fly, then we will load up. Once aboard, Chuck will get you in your initial stations and show you how the guns operate. Then we start engines, taxi out and take off and head right into the dawning sun at 090 degrees, just as so many did in the 40's. Any questions?"

Linda asked if they could all have a short prayer.

"Lord, continue to bless these friends as we all go now to honor those who have gone before us and did so much to retain our freedom and our way of life. Through them, we know it was for your Glory that they were able to triumph. As with any good thing you give us, thank you for this we are about to receive." All added 'Amen'.

As they went out to the tarmac, there was an excitement that was visible in the step, the chatter and the big smiles.

"Look at that beauty! She shines in the flood lights even! We are finally here!"

Mac gathered all at the nose under the "Gypsy Moth er" nose art, a magnificent young woman with a gypsy headdress, jewelry and little else. Rick noted the horizon lightening in the east. He could hardly believe he was there, getting ready to do a walk around on his B-17, preparing for a mission. How many times had this played out in England in the 1940's.

Linda asked what the story was behind the name, 'Gypsy Moth er".

Mac laughed, "The original name they came up with was "Gypsy Moth" because of the fact she had so many homes before 'Fantasy' got her and had, like her namesake, a voracious appetite for fuel since she was so poorly maintained and out of tune. Then after a while, we were informed that her name was used previously, something like 'nose art copyright'. Not wanting to make her a 'II', we just added the 'er' to make it Mother."

"Well, your subject is certainly beautiful, but hardly what you would consider as an image of 'motherly'"

When the laughter died down, Rick called everyone to attention and said,

"To Mother!" and they all saluted. After several crew shots, they began the customary 'walk around' check, done routinely by most pilots in the world before flight, with the possible exception of the old RAF, where, it was heard, consisted of 'Kick the tire and light the fire'.

The ground crew had previously given the Gypsy a thorough pre-flight, so this was more for familiarization than necessity.

As Mac and Chuck showed the bomb doors, the gun locations, all of interest to everyone, they all felt a kindred spirit with this assembly of steel and aluminum that was taking on an identity of it's own. They would touch it with an almost reverent manner when remembering all of the men who stood for them and did their duty in this, the embodiment of all the aircraft in that heroic time.

They checked the leading edges, the trailing edges, the surfaces as if all the souls the plane represented were right there. They imagined the view through the bubbles and windows of the turrets and nose and tail stations, always with the sense of 'what was it really like?' This was not a 'get on, read some, eat your peanuts and you're there. People were desperately trying to make sure you didn't make it back for another run at them. This was a time to honor those who didn't make it back and to thank those who did.

They began to get on board now and the level of anticipation went up a notch. Rick considered trying to pull himself up through the forward hatch but thought better of it. He decided it would be a foolish risk, especially on the brink of his dream come true. The thought of him having to nurse a strained muscle or joint damage on this flight was plenty to restore reason and to remind him that he was a long way from 20 years of age.

Entering was another experience. It was like going into the sanctuary of an old cathedral. That same reverence, not for the material structure, but for all the souls it represented. They were now in communion with family, friends and neighbors from a time gone by.

Chuck showed Bob and Sue their initial station in the tail gunner position. He explained where they were to sit on take-off and how to use the intercom. He explained the laser guns and how to defend us during the fighter attacks. Allen and Charlotte were at the waist gun positions, Ken and Marianne were to man the top turret. The ball turret was explained but no one would be in it, for several reasons, with comfort being a high priority reason.

Mac familiarized Rick and Linda with the nose gun and the bombardier/navigator position, then went up to the flight deck with Chuck. Chuck told them, 'fasten your seatbelts, we're about to start engines.' At last! Chuck made a quick check to be sure everyone was secured, then got back to the start procedure on the pre-flight check list. Rick felt a shiver of excitement as he heard 'one turning', and felt the vibration and heard the sound of the Wright Cyclone engine taking hold. Each engine in turn was brought to life until the Gypsy was humming with a strong pulse of 4,800 well-tuned horsepower

They saw a green light flash from the tower of the field and Gypsy moved out under the guidance of the ground crew. As she turned to the right, Rick heard the distinctive sound of the mechanical brakes, remembering that sound from the movies and air shows he had witnessed. This time, he was not just a witness, he was a part of it all. He was INSIDE! Linda was also taking all of this in and still, to her amazement, was really getting into it.

"Navigator to pilot".

"Go ahead, Rick".

"Mac, I just looked at this chart and saw the configuration of this field. The runways are laid out on a perfect cross pattern in the cardinal headings! How did that come about?"

"I don't know, Rick, but we're heading for runway 18 for take-off. This is different though. I haven't seen one like it before."

"The 360-180 runway is about 30% longer than the 90-270 and that east-west crosses about 1/3 of the way down from the north. Wonder what that is all about?"

"Rick, Mac, Bob here. My dad had told me about this field a long time ago. His dad, of course, had flown out of here and told him that, when the field was first opened, they had the Jennys and really didn't have marked runways, they just kept the whole field mowed. They just let the pilots choose their direction. After a while, they found that because of the prevailing winds and the trees and buildings around the field, these were the two paths that were worn with use, so they just hard-surfaced them just like they are today.

"Thanks for that, Bob. You know, I had a similar idea in college. The students had paths all over the campus, but not where the sidewalks were. My suggestion was to build the buildings and wait a year, then pave the paths, just like they did here."

"Yeah, that sounds like it would save lots of grass. Sounds like a patentable idea to me!"

They taxied toward the end of the runway, the tail wheel bouncing with the expansion joints in the taxiway. Rick thought that it would be considerably smoother if they had their full complement of 9 or 10 thousand pounds of bombs aboard. However, he was much happier that this load was sand bags!

Chapter IV

Takeoff!

Mac turned on to the runway and announced on the intercom, "Prepare for take-off".

Rick thought, 'All my life . . . '. The four Wright engines revved to a powerful roar and Gypsy started her roll. Increasing much faster than Rick had anticipated, he was reminded of the power this beauty had. He and Linda were watching the runway disappear beneath them, being pushed back into their seat webbing. Linda, to her most appreciated credit, was recording all of this on the video cam. Then, much sooner once more that Rick expected, the tail came up, then almost immediately Gypsy literally leaped into the air, yawing slightly to the left as a minor breeze had come up out of the southeast. It was countered quickly and she started to climb. At about 1,500 feet, they started a slow, climbing turn to the left to get on a heading of 090.

"Everybody okay?"

"Tail gunner okay"

"Waist guns okay"

"Top turret okay"

"Bombardiers okay"

"Hey, you guys ever do this before?"

"Nah, we just read a lot"

"You are something else! As soon as we reach our altitude, I'll let you know so you can get up and 'move about the cabin', as they say. Just don't fall out of the plane. Every time that happens it always makes our liability premium spike! And, keep your eyes open. Whenever it becomes known we are in an area, we are constantly 'attacked' by all sorts of aircraft. It guess it's good advertising, but it is embarrassing to be chased by a Cessna 150."

The morning was perfect. The sun was fully clear of the horizon now and the sky was clean of any blemish. Linda caught Venus being hidden behind the light of day as if it were trying to encroach on the sun's territory and stay out just a little longer. Ol' Sol would have no part of it and put her in her place.

"Rick, I think the sunrise we just captured will be worth checking for single prints. It was one of the most spectacular ones I have seen."

"This whole day is spectacular, well, maybe with the exception of the weird fog this morning. But, even that was spectacular."

"I know I've never seen anything like it."

"When we get back, I'm going to check with the weather guys and see what kind of conditions would have caused that."

"Look, we have an escort!"

"Mac, we have company. Port side, about 10 O'clock level, a beautiful AT-6"

"Yeah, I told you to watch. We seem to attract them."

"Got him, Linda?"

"Yeah, good thing I was quick . . . there he goes already. I caught his wing waggle and off he went."

"I bet he got hit with at least two lasers! Wonder why they didn't call him out in the back?"

"Guess they were looking in a different direction."

"Some defenders!"

"Mac, best I can figure from this chart and my 40 year plus old navigation skills, we should be about 10 minutes off the target. I just can't believe all of this!"

Rick was totally engrossed with the Norden bombsight.

"Linda, during the war you would have been shot on sight if you got too close to this and you weren't authorized. It was the key to precision bombing. Now look at it—practically a toy!"

Chuck had given them a quick schooling on what to do coming up on target. He was so ready for this.

"We've got to do this again! This isn't going to be enough! I can already tell."

"Rick, we just got started! Just settle down and enjoy what is happening right now. Do I need to remind you?"

"Oops! Sorry about that. It's easy to step back into old shoes. They're comfortable even though they are ugly and are bad for your 'soul'."

"Hey, that is pretty good! Okay, apology accepted."

"Thanks for that, angel. Now, let's get ready to score a shack on our run."

"A what?"

"Oh, uh, we're going to hit it dead on."

'Shack' sent Rick back to his early life in the Air Force and how ridiculous it always seemed to him that there was such an importance placed on the accuracy of a bomb drop, a dead center hit, within a few feet of the intended target was termed a 'shack'. What he didn't understand was that when you are dropping a weapon that, when detonated, immediately produced a fireball that was 25 miles in diameter, what's the fuss over a few feet? A few HUNDRED feet! He was then introduced to the concept of 'limited warfare', where there were politically correct rules of engagement, so you may be restricted to conventional weapons much like those used during World War II. This still made no sense to Rick. If you are pressed to armed conflict, use the best you have to end it as soon as possible! Unfortunately, his reasoning was not with the majority of the decision makers, though very popular with the crews.

Rick had taken his headset off to reach a pen he had dropped. He loved the sound the engines made as they bored through the air. Then, Linda touched his arm and motioned him to listen. He quickly replaced the headset and heard . . .

". . . something is wrong . . . can't . . . we all . . ."

Immediately Chuck went to the back. He was barely to the radio compartment when he called.

"Mac, we've got something going on here. Some seem to be sick or something. They . . . are . . . Mac . . . I'm . . ."

Nothing! They were wide-eyed, staring at each other. Rick called Mac,

"We're going back to check."

Both got out of their greenhouse and went to the middle of the aircraft. They were not prepared for what they saw. All of the crew were unconscious, including Chuck! They tried to wake him up, then tried all the rest, but could not get a response out of any of them. They all were breathing and their pulse was rapid and strong. They were all just completely unconscious . . . . ALL!!! . . . . They realized at the same time . . . . Mac!

They scrambled to the flight deck and sure enough, Mac was out like the rest of the crew! They would later recall the sheer panic they each felt at that moment. Rick tried to bring Mac around to no avail.

"We're in a slow turn. Seem to be stable. Linda, now is an unbelievably perfect time for a direct prayer! I'll start, but jump in anytime! Heavenly Father, we don't claim to know your will or what you have for us to learn in this present situation, but I know that you are aware of our predicament and also that we are way over our heads here and need your special help here. We don't need to know your reason, just please help us to do something to help our friends back there. We are totally in your hands. Your will be done."

Linda said 'Amen'.

"Hon, I can't add to that."

"Okay, darlin', now let's see what He wants us to do. First thing we've got to do is to get Gypsy under some kind of control. Angel, you're gonna have to fly for a minute while I get Mac out of that seat. His feet are fouling the rudder pedals. Go ahead and get into the co-pilot seat and strap in. Do you feel the pedals there?"

"Yeah, I'm a bit short of them, but I can reach them."

"Okay, there should be a seat adjustment like on a car . . . there . . . now, how is that?"

"That's good, I can reach them fine now, for whatever good that will do!"

"Okay, here's your flying class from one who knows nothing! You push the left pedal if you want to go left, the right one to go right. The yoke, you turn the wheel left, you bank the plane to the left. Push the whole yoke forward to put the nose down, pull it back to climb—that's all I know about it! Talk about trusting in the Lord!!! Just try to keep it steady and upright and at this same altitude, pointing to the altimeter, and heading, pointing to the compass, of 090. You shouldn't have to touch the throttles."

"How long are you going to be gone? Sounds like you are going out to lunch!"

"I'll get him back and strapped in and be right back as fast as I can. Then, God only knows what."

He dragged Mac out of the seat and back to the first webbed jump seat. He got him up and tried to strap him in. About that same time, Allen Collier slumped out of his seat and on to the floor. Rick jumped to help him, got him up and back in his seat and strapped in. He looked around quickly trying to assess the rest of the crew. Then there were some erratic movements of the plane! He jumped back up to the flight deck and got into the pilot seat.

"Having a problem, the obvious not considered?"

"You might have noticed, I tried the controls to see what they all did. Rick, I was gripping that yoke so hard I was losing feeling in my hands. I moved the controls around and that seemed to relax my hands some."

Rick was in awe.

"You won't have to, but remind me when we get down to tell you what an incredible woman you are! Right now, I'm going to try to turn us around and head back to the base. If we head 270, we should be somewhere close in about 20 minutes. We'll try to figure out what to do on the way back. I wish I knew more about the radio in this thing. The original was just behind the flight deck . . . . wait . . . here is a control. On, and now I'll try the channel selector . . . not even static! Okay, we're turning around! Linda, we're going to do this. Watch the altimeter and make sure I don't lose altitude in the turn. I'll watch for other traffic. You ready?"

"Ready as I'll ever be. Let's do this before I realize what is happening."

"Okay, here goes!"

He banked the plane to the left slightly with a little left rudder and back pressure on the yoke and the magnificent Gypsy started a slow turn to the left.

After what seemed to Rick an eternity, he completed what he would later describe as the sloppiest turn ever made in a B-17. Right now, however, they were after results so technique would have to settle for a distant second. They came around to a heading of 270.

"Rick, how ya doing?"

"Well, tough as that was, I'm afraid that was the easy part. Now what? So we get to the field, then what? I don't see a way I could successfully land this thing and it's not just us. There are eight others depending on what we do!"

"We wanted excitement! What's that old saw about being careful what you ask for?"

"Cute! You know a preposition is a bad thing to end a sentence with!"

Rick went through the radio controls again.

"Not even static. Linda, if this wasn't so near putting us into shock, this would be the most incredible experience of my life! It still may be, but I can't get past that panic that is just below the surface!"

"Well, we have to put it where it belongs, in Jesus' Hands, so somehow it will work out for His Glory and our benefit."

"I know He is always with us, but this time I wouldn't blame Him a bit if He waited on the ground!"

"Rick, when you were in back, I was scared out of my wits . . . me, of all people, barely able to ride in a plane, up here by myself, actually flying this one and, as you mentioned, all of us depending on me to do it right! My mind was racing, approaching panic. I know better, but for a second, I forgot that I was never by myself. I was sent a message to remind me though. The sun was reflecting through a window in such a way that it made a perfect cross right there on the panel! That was when I got that shot of inner strength and decided to try my wings, so to speak. You know what? We're going to be just fine with all of this. That message told me all I needed to know that help was indeed here."

"I agree that one way or another, we're going to be just fine. I am sure that the crew is in the same 'win, win' situation we're in. I'm trying this radio one more time."

He switched through all the channels, still not a sound. He tried 'mayday' on every one of them and no response anywhere.

"I don't even know if this plane has a transponder. If I were more comfortable with the controls, I could try the triangle pattern to let ground control radar know we had a problem. I think we just need to get back to the base. The ground crew there will know we have a problem when we come back so early."

"You sure you've never done this before? That's a great idea."

"Linda, I'm pretty sure this lever lowers the landing gear. It would probably be better for us to land wheels up in the grass"

"Not after watching that landing in "12 O'clock High"."

"I know. That image is right in front of my mind."

"Do you think, I mean, you did land that Cessna 150 enough to be able to do it okay, right?"

"That was a tricycle gear, light, not even in the same league, no comparison at all."

"Do you think we can get this one down?"

"Oh, it'll come down . . . that's not the problem . . . it will come down by itself. The key here is that we are able to walk away from it after it is down. I don't even know about the flaps, don't know the stall speed, there's just nothing to draw in my limited experience."

"Well, it's all we have and it will have to be enough."

"One thing about it, we're in a position where we have to try it. In our case, God is the Pilot and we are the co-pilots. Talk about coming in on a wing and a prayer. Look at us! Here we are, flying this plane and quite well, I might add, heading where we want to go and we haven't lost any altitude, so in spite of the problems, so far, we are doing okay."

"The present urgency is those sick folks in the back. It sure seems to be something they got into before we got there. Sue did mention that the eggs didn't taste quite right to her, but they all ate them anyway. Maybe some kind of food poisoning."

"Yeah, they seemed stable, but the unconsciousness part is not good, so the quicker we can get them help the better. I sure wished that radio worked. I bet there isn't a cell phone anywhere and you know everyone has one. But, who would even think about bringing one or even wanting one on this trip?"

"We're in it and we'll go with the One who always gets us through, however He wants to do it.

"Amen to that!"

Rick looked back to see Mac slumping out of his seat.

"I never got Mac strapped in before Allen went down! Are you okay with being here while I take care of him?"

"Yeah, but hurry back. I don't want to look back there and see you playing with one of the guns!"

"Be right back, angel."

Rick made a mental note of the sight of Linda flying this plane, with that determined look on her face that said she was giving it all she had, a memory he would cherish as long as he lived . . . . however long that might be.

As he got to Mac, Rick tried to bring him around again but he was out cold. He noted again that Mac seemed stable but just with that elevated pulse. Wait a minute . . . would food poisoning raise heart rate? Cause unconsciousness? What are you talking about that for? It doesn't matter at this point, he's out! He got Mac back into the seat and strapped him in this time. He looked out the right waist window and saw that they went into a cloud. This cloud was something he had never seen before, weirdly colored, like mother-of-pearl. They came right out of it in just a moment, for which Rick was grateful. They didn't need a visibility problem with what they already had on their plate. He went back to the flight deck to check on Linda.

"Ma'am, the passengers want to know what's going to be on the menu for lunch."

She did manage a chuckle.

"Is everybody okay back there?"

"Well, if you are doing as well as it appears that you are, I'll go do a thorough check and make sure they are as prepared as we can get them for whatever kind of landing we come up with."

"Okay, but again, don't get lost back there. I don't want you to miss anything up here!"

"Yes dear, I'll be right back."

Rick had just checked the belts of the last one when there were four quick, heavy thumps and the plane banked sharply to the right.

"What now?"

He scrambled to the flight deck and found Linda leveling the plane like a seasoned veteran. She was yelling,

"He tackied up my plane!"

"Who? What happened? What are you talking about?"

"There! He did it!"

She was pointing to a yellow-nosed black fighter with full Nazi battle dress, coming up in front and banking around to the right.

"Linda, that is a Focke-Wulf 190!"

"I don't care what it is, look at what he did to my wing!"

Just beyond the outboard engine there were four jagged holes in the wing!

"What is going on here?"

Rick was now in the pilot seat and barely able to breathe, thinking that surely this wasn't a part of the show — those holes are the real thing!

"He's coming around again! Rick, I never saw him before he shot us and dived by!"

She picked up the video camera and started it.

"I'm going to get this on record so if we crash, maybe somebody will find it and see what happened to us!"

She was almost out of the window with her camera going. Rick was stunned and immobile!

"This cannot be happening! It's just not possible!"

He snapped back to reality and tried the radio again— still nothing!

"If we just had a cell phone."

He couldn't think of a beneficial reason to try evasive maneuvering, especially since 'straight and level' was their long suit right now.

Linda yelled that he was closing again and they were going to be hit.

"Wish we had something to shoot back other than this camera!"

Rick watched and heard himself mumbling, 'why isn't he firing? He's got to be in range!'

They both jumped at the sudden sound of gunfire coming from their plane! They looked back to see the right waist gunner in battle gear and the lower torso of the top turret gunner, both firing right into the surprised 190! Linda had looked back with her camera going and caught the action. Rick could only mutter that 'Rod Serling must be close by'. Linda turned back to the fighter coming in to see the tracers marking a stream of bullets going right into it, pieces of glass and metal flying off the plane. It banked sharply to get its armor-plated belly into the path of the incoming .50 caliber bullets, but it was too late. Smoke filled the cockpit and flames came from under the engine. It was spiraling down now. A figure separated from the burning plane as Linda continued to follow it down with the cam. A chute opened shortly after that. Rick, fighting shock, managed to say,

"Linda, it is April 16, 2004. We are the only conscious people in a B-17 that we are flying and know nothing about how to fly it, and somehow, our plane has just been attacked and damaged by a Luftwaffe Focke-Wulf 190, then again, somehow, our plane shot that fighter down!!! How? The guns are plugged . . . as if that mattered, who fired them??"

Linda looked back and saw a familiar face at the right waist gun. He smiled and gave her a 'thumbs up' victory sign. She tapped Rick on the arm to look, but then there was no one there!

"Rick, what was Uncle Ned's position on the B-17?"

"He was the right waist gunner/radio man. Why?"

"Rick, he still IS! I know that was him! So young, but that was him! I couldn't see the face of the one in the top turret, but someone was definitely there. The shell casings were raining down from there, too."

"There's no way! Those guns were plugged and were never armed, only with the lasers!"

"You saw it, I saw it and we have it on video!"

Rick was looking ahead now, noticing that they were over water. In the distance, there they were! Unmistakably, a sight so familiar to returning airmen in the 1940's, the white cliffs of Dover! Somehow, they were now over the English Channel, headed for England! Rick's only thought at the moment was that he had quit smoking too soon. He seemed to go in and out of reality, not knowing which he was most confused.

He was brought back to reality by the sound and sight of the #4 engine first running rough, then smoking and bursting into flame

"Oh, good! Another opportunity to build character! I had hoped we were pretty well built out on this project. Lord, here I am again, as You can see, we're having a tough time just keeping sane here so please feel free to step in any time now! Linda, we've got to snuff that fire. There are fire extinguishers for each engine on the upper panel, see the one for #4? Yeah, I believe that is it. Okay, I'm shutting it down . . . . Well, it's still burning! Okay, pull that lever . . . hold it . . . . good, that knocked it down some . . . . watch it and if it flares up again, we'll just try it again. It's still smoking . . . he hit us harder than I thought. I think I'm supposed to increase the power to these other engines to maintain cruise speed, so here goes . . . . okay, there is 150 again. I believe we can go just fine on the three left."

"Go where, Rick?"

"I know, we're heading for England and only God knows how we're doing that, but the destination, however incredible, really doesn't matter, since we are still in the same fix. When we get wherever we're heading or just run out of fuel, how are we gonna get this lady down on the ground upright?"

"Rick, here it is, we're going to do what He has planned for us, and whatever it is, it will be what He wants us to do. How bad is that?"

"Sounds simple when you say it fast. I know you're right. I guess all those folks in the back are on out ticket, too. Okay, I guess we'll look for the first landing field and go from there". At once, there was a sight he recognized.

"Linda, look just ahead! There's a cloud like the one we went through earlier!"

"I've got it! What a beautiful color."

They went through the cloud and immediately into the clear, bright sunlight again. Now the cliffs were gone, the channel, also.

". . . just can't handle this . . ."

They didn't have time to think about that or anything that had just happened, because straight ahead was the same Foster Field they had left earlier.

"Linda, I've got to be the worst navigator . . . we came back after the turn-around by way of Europe and in the 1940's!"

"Well, now we have to figure out how to get these folks down safely and get them some help. We've got plenty to think about and talk over, but later."

Rick gave the radio another try . . . . nothing! In disgust, he took off his headset and began to try to locate flaps, landing gear switches, throttles, and it all looked so foreign, absolutely nothing to relate to the controls of the J-3 Cub or the Cessna 150!

"My God, help me!"

Linda jumped and quickly grabbed her headset and held it close to her ears, motioning for Rick to get his back on as she was saying,

"Go ahead, and are we glad to hear you!"

Rick was on and listening to the most wonderful sound he could imagine at that time—an authoritative voice, calm and in total control.

"Youall are doing fine, just great . . . I'm going to bring you in on a direct approach to save time. Emergency vehicles are already on the field for your friends, so just settle back and relax. Sorry, that's not even funny, I know, but I can assure you that you are in very capable hands and we'll have you on the ground safely in a few minutes. I will give you each what needs to be done, so just follow my lead. Rick, ease back on the throttles, keep that mixture a little rich." Rick reached up and pulled the throttles back until the voice said,

"That's just right. Now, Linda, push the landing gear lever down . . . that's it . . . . good. Now, the flaps down to the ¼ mark."

Linda seemed to know instinctively that the controls were the right ones, a mental note for later.

"Rick, line up on runway 27, since we have a west wind, we are going with the short runway, but it is plenty long enough. Point the nose at the first foot of concrete of that runway. Linda, give me ½ flaps now and Rick, keep the nose on that end of the runway. Youall are doing so well."

Rick started, "but what . . ."

"Just listen, we'll discuss later. Linda, full flaps now, Rick keep the nose on that spot. The wind is right down the runway, so this should be a 'breeze'—pardon, couldn't resist that one!"

Rick glanced at Linda, noting how she was gripping that yoke and the determined set expression on her face—what a woman God had entrusted to him—a blessing he knew he didn't deserve—another example of the Father's Grace.

"You're drifting a bit . . . stay with me."

"Sorry, I was distracted for a second."

"I understand and agree that you are truly blessed."

Rick thought, "How did he know . . ."

"Okay, when I tell you, both of you ease back on the yoke until I say stop. You will flare, settle and the main gear will touch. Okay, get ready . . . over the runway, now ease back, more, more, okay . . . hold . . . hold . . . hold."

Rick thought they were too high to be flaring out, but thought he had better trust that voice over what he felt, so he did as directed. They flared out and settled smoothly, the right wing dipping some. The right landing gear touched first, then the left and they stuck, settling easily. They were instructed to ease the tail down, cut the throttles and to apply the brakes smoothly. The voice said,

"Great job, you two! I'm really proud of you both! And, I want to thank you personally for what you did for my Gypsy!"

They rolled to a stop and Linda shut the engines down, wondering how she knew how to do that. The plane had barely stopped when it was surrounded by the anxious ground crew, four ambulances, a fire truck, an FAA vehicle and a USAF staff car.

Just before Rick took off his headset, the voice came back on,

"One of my crew wants to say 'hi' to you. Another voice, more familiar, said,

"Nice landing, Woo Woo!"

Linda said, "That's him, Rick! Only one of your uncles would call you 'Woo Woo'!

They called him that after an old comic strip character, Woo Woo Wortle, the boy who was never spanked.

"Rick, I knew that was him at the gun station!"

He had died in 1998.

They sat there staring straight ahead, in a daze. The ground crew opened the door and the emergency team began assessing the unconscious and removing them from the plane to the waiting ambulances. The FAA and Air Force contingent were intently studying the battle damage.

"Linda, not a shadow of doubt that Jesus is involved in all of this. I can't quite get my mind around it all right now, but you and I both know that we have been let in on something incredible and I just want to be able to use it all as He intends."

"Well, He got us this far into it, so I don't think it is likely that He will leave us out here to flounder around."

"So many questions, though . . . where did all these people hear about our problem? Who would have told them the details? Just can't think right now."

Chapter V

Aftershock

One of the EMT's came up to them and asked if they were both okay. They just stared at him! He did congratulate them on an excellent landing, making the tired old remark about 'any you can walk away from is good'. He checked their vital signs then escorted them out of the cockpit. Rick bumped into the yoke while getting out of his seat and felt the old Air Corp bible in his jacket pocket.

"Well, it had one more blessing in it for sure" he thought to himself out loud.

"Sir?"

"Nothing. I was just thanking God for the ride."

He noticed he and Linda were both a bit shaky in the legs when they got to the ground. They kneeled and thanked God for their safe delivery and prayed for healing for their friends.

Just before getting into the ambulance, Rick called 'attention' and they saluted their 'Gypsy'.

Under close supervision, the FAA had the ground crew move the plane to the apron, secure it and cordon it off. They stationed Air Police guards at each end of the plane. Linda had pointed it out to Rick that they were taking such care with Gypsy, but neither could bring themselves to comment on it, just able to look and point. They were taken to the hospital for a thorough examination, and since they were still in mild shock, they were admitted to be kept overnight for observation. Linda called the family to let them know where they were and that they were fine and would be home tomorrow. She then called Phil and Edith to fill them in also and to ask if they would check on Captain again for them. They of course agreed and said they would be glad to do it and check on their place as well. Edith said that word of their experience was already out but details were too sketchy to know what had happened and that they couldn't wait to hear this story!

"Who told people about this?"

They were checked again and told to get some rest for now. Also, as they could probably imagine, there were several 'officials' that were most anxious to talk with them, but rest was the top priority for them and they would not be disturbed. They were still not able to talk about 'things' even among themselves, so they just held each other and went into a strange sleep.

The next morning they felt better, though still a little numb. After they were checked over again, they were brought breakfast and then checked one more time by one they both suspected to be from the Air Force Space Medicine Team. Then they were released.

Their first priority was to locate Mrs. Johnson's room and visit with her.

"How are you today?"

"Oh, I'm a little sore, but much better. It is so nice of youall to come see me! I've been walking around some and they seem to like how I have improved, so maybe I can get out of here soon."

"That sounds really good. Captain is doing fine, but he does miss you. We were just close by and wanted to check on you."

After a short visit, they left and went back to the lobby where they were met by one of the Doctors and asked if they would feel up to talking to some folks who were about to 'pop', as he put it, to talk to them.

"We knew that was coming and we, I believe, are ready to see them."

They went into the main meeting room there in the hospital annex and were ushered into the room. Representatives were there waiting for them. The FAA was there, the Air Force, and some they didn't recognize from the party present yesterday at their landing.

Frank Thompson with the FAA introduced himself and the others there and apologized to them for hitting them so soon after their ordeal, but stressed the importance of learning the details of what they had experienced.

"So, with your kind indulgence, please tell us everything from your first encounter with the information about this flight to how it developed and in as much detail as you can recall about the actual flight."

They allowed that they would normally interview the main sources separately to corroborate each story, but in this case they chose to do that with the rest of the crew but to talk to Rick and Linda together as every minute detail of this fantastic story was so important.

"First, how are our friends?"

"Oh, they are all doing well. We don't have all the reports on them just yet, but the preliminary tests indicate some kind of food poisoning."

Rick asked if they could have some coffee since this would take some time.

When they got the coffee, they held hands and began to relate this episode from the 'wake-up call', the radio ad, the brochure in the paper, the fact that nobody on the block got that insert but them, on through the whole amazing course of events to the miraculous landing. It seemed so strange to be relating this story to so many extremely interested people. The interviewees asked few questions, having recorded the entire talk, but Rick remembered later that they all made special notes about the color and make-up of the cloud, the video cam Linda used and for some reason, the position as best as they could place it where they had seen the white cliffs of Dover. They were most interested, however, in the fighter attack, especially that Linda had filmed it on the video cam. Also of major interest was the shot of the B-17 guns actually firing at the attacking fighter, and of course, the voice guiding them to their landing,

They were all so predisposed that they almost left without thanking Rick and Linda for the information. As they all apologized again, they said 'we will talk again'.

"This is some story"

To say the least!!

Rick and Linda were given a ride back to the air field to retrieve the car. They saw now that Gypsy was inside the hangar, still secured. The ride home was quiet, still being overwhelmed by all that had happened, especially just going over it, which seemed to make it more incredible.

When they got home, they called the family and let all know they were back and would get together with everyone as soon as they unwound. They made a pot of French roast coffee and got into the hot tub. Then, as they were starting to relax, they were able to talk about it all.

"Rick, what would have happened if it were not for that fog?"

"Well, I guess we would have all been a part of Gypsy in the most literal sense of the word. You may not have—you probably wouldn't have eaten the eggs, if it turns out to be that was the culprit. Then it would have been all you by yourself."

"My God in heaven! I can't even think about that!"

"Well, you know, with the Pilot we had, I think you would have done just great. We would have missed those invaluable pictures everyone is so excited about though"

"I still don't want to think abut that happening!"

"I would like to find the guy who talked us down."

"You know, I've been thinking about that, too. Rick, he was right there with us in that cockpit . . . who called in for assistance for us at the field? . . . . I think we will find out who that was, IS, when we see Ned again!"

"I can't figure any other explanation either. I can't help wanting to know who he was, IS!"

"Rick, when we went through that cloud the first time, there was no change in the light, the sun was behind us, no change in haze, the only thing I noticed was maybe a change in the landscape, but even that was 'spring green' all over."

"Yeah, I remember being so thankful that we ran out of it so quickly."

"You know, when that fighter attacked us, it was so sudden I almost jumped out of the seat. He dived right by us after he shot those holes in my beautiful wing. I could see his face, Rick. He was staring right at me."

"I couldn't grasp what you were telling me when I got there. I could see it was a FW190 and I remembered Mac telling us there would be attacks coming off the bomb run, but they would be by a Messerschmidt 109. Just couldn't get it all to gel, especially with those holes in the wing and the engine smoking."

"Rick, I just thought—both you and Phil had dreams about you and I flying that plane! What do you think of that!

"Yeah, that's right. Wait until he hears about that!

As the warm water and hot coffee relaxed the body and soul, the memories came flooding back to both of them. No detail of the event was lost in the replay as both minds were activated as one.

"Rick, do you recall me almost hanging out the window with the video camera filming as he made a run at us again? Why wasn't I trying to get under the seat!"

"That's no weirder that I was, acting as his gunnery instructor, questioning as to why he wasn't firing as he was well within range. For a quick minute, I thought the first pass was some kind of mistake, but about then our 'gunners' started firing! Watching those tracers going into that plane, I knew that was the real thing!"

"When I looked back, there was only Ned at the waist gun and I could see legs from the top turret and I got them on the video cam. I can't wait to see what shows up on that."

"How in the world did you recover that plane so quickly when we were hit?"

"I just thought about what you said about turning the wheel, so I just slowly turned it to the left and it came right back upright, but it was as if I had power steering this time. Rick, I know I had help with that and I do believe that 'help' would have righted the Gypsy with or without me. Talk about a grip on the yoke, I bet my finger marks are still on it!"

"We both had every reason to panic and just lose it, but there was just something like a blanket of 'okay' over us—you saw the sign earlier . . . this is so incredible! We should write all this down before we forget something."

"Well, they already recorded enough of our initial interview that I'm sure we can recall the details that go with that transcript."

"Rick, I recorded that fighter from just prior to our guns firing at him to as far as I could see it going in on fire. Now, I don't know a lot about this sort of thing, but watching those bullets tearing out bits of metal and glass, especially in the cockpit area, how was that pilot able to get out of it and open his parachute?"

"I just don't know. We're way over our heads here, but I do believe that, as Sherlock would say, 'all will be revealed'"

"Okay, then what is all this about the English Channel and the White cliffs of Dover? Were we in some kind of virtual reality experiment or did we jump into another dimension or time warp? Then, just as quickly, there we were back on track to the field! And, I'm with you about where the guy was that talked us down if not in the Spirit world? He had access to us somehow."

"I know one time, when we were coming in for the landing, I was looking at you, kinda in a daze, and he knew it!"

"I remember—he told you to stay with him! Could there be a camera in the cockpit?" "I don't know that either. All I know is that I never landed that 150 any better than how well he got us down with Gypsy! There was no way I could have done that without his prompting. Looking back, I would have flown us right into the ground before I tried to flare out! It just seemed that we were way too high! I think we both know there is something so much bigger here, not just the Supernatural happenings, but I think He has allowed all this to happen as a part of some plan. I just can't imagine what it could be. Why put us through all this, the sickness, the stress overload, what can be made from all that? Was it all a severe test of Faith? No doubt we would all have been killed without Divine Intervention."

"Could it have been some kind of alien abduction? That reminds me of Richard T. Gonzales. Remember him, old Speedy? He told me about a time when he was a kid in San Antonio and all the family children were in the back yard when they saw some kind of object above them. The others ran in the house but Richard stayed out and watched it. The next thing he remembered was in the exact same place and it was dark. The family had called the police and all the neighbors had been searching for him all afternoon. Nobody has explained that as yet."

"We need Vicki here. She is the one who has the experience of the spirit world! She has had numerous visits that could not be explained and is definitely in tuned whether she wants it or not."

"Whoever the voice was and wherever he came from, it was from God. We had to be in the Spiritual Realm."

"Yeah, but why? Not a very convincing sign for skeptics. I guess a highly skilled pilot could have talked us down without any supernatural involvement, but it would have taken a whole lot of good luck!"

"Okay, given the miracle of the landing could possibly be explained, how about the attack on us and the holes in our wing?"

"That's another one we aren't equipped to answer. I guess some terrorist could have really attacked us with live ammunition, but what in the world for? I'm not even going to get into the guns firing that were plugged and seeing the fighter going down in flames."

"We've got to get that video cam! I bet it has already been gone over with every tool they have! I can't wait to see what you got on that! The more we get into this, the more wound up I am getting! Did you get the cloud and . . ."

"Yes, and the white cliffs of Dover! How is that to be explained?"

"Hey, I'm still working on the fog lifting!"

They just sat there for a long time, trying to think clearly about what had transpired and what the reason for it could be.

"I'm at the end of this for now, but I do feel that the Lord will feed us what we can handle when we can take it. He knows we are practically in overload right now, so we'll get it when it's time."

"Rick, I've always believed we could interact with those who have gone before us, especially family. What are angels but spiritual messengers from God. Now, obviously we know they can be in any form needed to do His Work. They, according to the Bible, are intelligent beings existing beyond the space-time dimensions of our universe. They are of course, subject to God's spiritual laws, but not to all of earth's natural laws."

"Yeah, this same Bible talks about a God who acts outside our pitiful realm and sure isn't restricted to any of the cosmic space-time dimensions. After all, He created them! I'm with you all the way on this. You know I have talked about, once we are in His Kingdom, going back in time and 'witnessing' events we can choose to see. Well, I guess this whole thing proves that we can, when the conditions allow, access other dimensions beyond what we can even imagine! It tells me that, when we get there, we can witness all the mysteries of this old earth. I want to see that asteroid that hit the gulf of Mexico and watch the pyramids being built, so much more."

"Don't you think there will be limits?"

"Why would there be? We wouldn't be able to change anything, just observe."

"What about that plane our crew shot down yesterday?"

". . . . okay, I may not be quite as ready as I thought for 'extra-dimensional theories'. Remember, this is only a $1.37 brain. But, even with my limitations, I want to know more. Let's get out of here before we prune up."

Linda called Phil and Edith. "Can you come over for some coffee and the most amazing story you've ever heard? Rick, they said they were pretty covered up right now but would see what they could work in and immediately hung up!"

They live three minutes away and were there in two.

"Wonder who that could be? Linda, look who is here!

So glad you could work us in on such short notice!"

"Well, we really weren't that busy, so . . . Had quite an experience, did you?"

"Phil, we actually flew that plane, just like you saw in the dream! Not by choice, mind you, but we were right where you had seen us!"

They all got coffee and went into the den, all on the edge of the seats.

"You already know about the wake-up call, which by the way, the other three couples got the same thing at the same time."

Then both began to relate the happenings from that point, from the fog delay right through the miracle landing. Phil was especially interested in the apparition of the real crew and the voice that had so precisely guided them down.

"Rick, I met your uncle if you recall and that was a long time ago, when we were kids, but I sure do still remember him. Tell me again what the voice said after you were down."

"He said, 'Great job, you two. I want to personally thank you both for all you have done for my Gypsy.'"

"Sounds to me like he was the A/C of your uncle's plane. If you could find anything on that crew, that would be my best guess as to who he was—IS."

"Yeah, he sure is still very protective of his Gypsy! I bet he was steamed about that 190 shooting holes in her wing. I will check with my cousins and see if Ned had any pictures around there with that crew. He didn't keep much of that kind of thing. I remember seeing what had happened to his A-2 jacket and I almost cried. He let me keep it for a while when I was a kid and I wore it like the highest honor that could have been bestowed on me. Anyway, I will check into it. I would sure like to know."

"This whole thing is just mind-blowing. The part about going through the cloud that was a time portal, that's what we read about in sci-fi, not to expect it in real life!"

"We sure understand what you are saying. We don't believe it sometimes and we went through it! How or why it happened, we just don't know, but we know this for certain . . . we have been chosen to be a part of this and are in for the whole ride. It is like being given the answer to an age-old problem but we haven't been given the problem! I do feel that we will all be given what we are supposed to know when the time is according to His plan for us. At least, that is what we're praying to happen."

"By the way, we did see Mrs. Johnson at the hospital. She will be home tomorrow. We told her that Captain was fine—hope that was accurate."

"Oh, he's great. We're both fast friends with him now. She's such a neat lady and we both feel so guilty about not checking on her much sooner."

"We're all in the same neighborhood, my friends, so we are in the same boat."

"We'll make it up to her when she gets back."

"Okay, we're going now and let you relax. We've got plenty to think about and discuss after we try to digest all of this. Thank you for including us in this amazing experience."

"I think you were included when you were given that 'vision'. I don't think we need to tell you that this is something way out of the ordinary and it gives me shivers of excitement to feel that we are involved with something that not many could even imagine."

"I know that and feel the same way. Can you believe we are living something like this in this present time? Who says the age of miracles is past. All I can say is thank God for letting us be in on it."

Chapter VI

Debriefing

Next morning they had decided to get everyone together and talk this out. They felt sure the others were as anxious as they about it. Rick called Mac on his cell phone since he had no idea where he might be.

"Mac, this is Rick. Just wanted to check in and see how you and Chuck are doing. We were able to talk to the others but have been missing catching you."

"Oh, we are fine now, thanks for asking. We've been a bit busy, as you can imagine, with meetings and such."

"Yeah, I can imagine. We were wanting to get everyone for a talk session."

"Funny you should mention that, well, not really, since this sort of thing has become the norm. I was getting ready to give you a call to arrange that very thing. How does tomorrow, about 10 am at the Federal building sound?"

"Sounds okay but ominous. The Federal building?"

"The FAA has their regional office there and it's a good central location. The whole gang will be there. Rick, we've got a real stir going and I can't help but be tickled to death about it and to be in on it. It is a delight for me to see these guys walking around talking to themselves."

"I do understand. Linda and I are in with them in that respect."

"The Air Force has been pretty busy on this as well. I don't know what all they have been up to, but the guys tell me that they have put in some overtime since Saturday and isn't letting up. Actually Chuck and I have become real close to the owner of Fantasy Flights, too. You might say we have had constant contact. Anyway, plan on a session Tuesday. There will be much to hear and discuss."

"Thanks, Mac. We're both looking forward to it and seeing everybody again. We've experienced something that I'm not sure anybody has ever come close to before, so I consider us a unique club."

"Rick, as the saying goes, 'you ain't seen nuttin' yet! See you tomorrow."

"Linda, we don't have anything on for tomorrow morning do we?"

"What's going on?"

"Mac says we're all having a reunion tomorrow morning at 10am at the FAA office in town."

"You bet we can make it! Besides, I want to see everybody again."

"Yeah, can you imagine me telling him we just couldn't make it because of a bridge tournament conflict?"

"I think we would be 'escorted' there from the level of security we saw."

"Don't let me forget to ask if all this is to be written up when it is all pulled together. Won't that be a great read!"

"Well, you can be sure that with the Fed involved there will be volumes of paper generated. Remember that rule that they go by; the report is complete when the weight of the paper generated equals that of the generator."

"I am surprised we are getting together so soon. It's going to be quite a day!"

The day arrived clear and cool. When they arrived at the Federal building, the 'coolness' was somewhat tarnished. Having to go through the metal detectors and the scrutiny of the now-commonplace security system, Rick couldn't help but feel another tug at his heart for the good ol' days, before all this became the necessity it was. They found and entered the FAA office complex and were ushered into a meeting room with a large semi-circular table, reminding them of the 'hot seat' arrangement where some poor soul sat in the center of the group and was grilled from all sides. However, when they saw everybody from the crew, it was old home week! After much hugging and hand shaking and 'how are you feeling now', they all took their seats at the table. This time there was nobody on the 'hot seat'. They were all where they could see each other as they talked over their experience.

Bill Fisher, the regional director of the FAA office, introduced himself and welcomed everyone, thanking them for making the time to be there. He assured them that all would find that the information assembled there would be well worth any inconvenience to them.

"Since this is my office, I get to lead off!", bringing laughs to stave off any anticipation of all business at this meeting.

"Our part of this puzzle consisted of the standard monitoring of the previously filed flight plan for your flight. Our air traffic controllers monitored and, by the way, recorded your flight by radar from the time you left Foster Field space through your turn around and heading back toward the field. At a point, we lost radar contact for a period of 4 minutes 37 seconds. During this time, there were attempts made for radio contact to no avail. There was additional traffic in your vicinity, above and below your last position, that was in constant radar contact and no one reported visual contact until we got you back. At that time, we had two visual reports, both agreeing that, one second there was nothing, then, there you were. Both mentioned a cloud resembling mother-of-pearl in color in your track, but nothing else in the area.

A B-17 is pretty obvious in our current air traffic and draws a lot of attention, but no one saw it for just over 4 ½ minutes. Your flight came back on radar just five miles from the field. Now while that disappearance is a major mystery in itself, the radio is something else. And, I might add, even more baffling. The radio in the Gypsy had been removed for repair and, while the normal procedure is to have a backup installed before a commercial flight, in this case both Mac and Chuck had fully operational radios in their jackets. The intercom was separate from the radio so the pilot or co-pilot could talk to the passengers without blocking the radio. Of course, Rick and Linda missed that part of the briefing so were unaware of that."

"Linda, there were radios there all the time!"

"The mystery is, of course, how did they talk you down on non-existent radios? I will interject here that you both did a miraculous job of landing."

"No wonder we couldn't get the thing to work! Wait, it DID work! It was loud and clear! Linda, I need an alka-seltzer!"

The laughter was a release and an affirmation that this was the way this whole thing would be going. It was as if to say, 'bring on some more'!

More came. Mac got up next and immediately thanked Rick and Linda for all of them. All gave a rousing ovation. Linda thanked everyone, but quickly added that they were all aware as to where the thanks should be directed.

"We did nothing but follow His direction, and there is no question in either of our minds that we would have all been statistics if left to us alone to get Gypsy down, so, thank you, Lord!"

More applause and 'Amens'.

Mac said that it was so far beyond him that he could only join them in that ovation.

"However it happened, I know it happened just a you said. When the ground crew was allowed to go into the plane, they picked up 66 .50 caliber shell casings. Folks, those guns were plugged and completely inoperative except for the laser transmitter added on! They could, well, let me correct that, they SHOULD not have been able to fire under any circumstance."

Colonel Edwin Boggs then got up to give the Air Force report.

"As you crew members know, each was interviewed separately as is the SOP for anything that may prove to be controversial. Needless to say, these events are 'highly qualified'! You have already been told about the shell casings, which were I might add, made in 1944, and had been most recently fired. I know, how? The holes are consistent with damage caused by the cannon armament of the FW190. Now, if that wasn't enough, we retrieved the video camera that you left on the plane and, I'll take full responsibility for viewing it without your permission, but I deemed it totally appropriate in lieu of the nature of this investigation."

"Of course it is okay with us, but was there any good stuff we can keep?"

"It is certainly your property. We did take another liberty and copied it, but the original is yours and you just can't imagine how important it is. The footage, I guess you call it, that Linda took is incredible in its' clarity. It shows in detail the 190. From those images, we were able to retrieve numbers from it and with the help of Luftwaffe archives we determined the plane was shot down on April 16, 1944! That is 60 years to the day before your flight. We were further able to corroborate the time by continuing with the video. As Linda followed the plane down, she inadvertently filmed the Richter Radar complex just below them, completely intact and functional. This array was a high priority target just before D-day and was totally destroyed on April 17, 1944 and never rebuilt. Another amazing confirmation showed the 'original' waist gunner firing and there were Bob and Sue Foster and Allen Collier all strapped in their jump seats and obviously unconscious!

Now, in my experience, an investigation should answer some of the original questions that prompted it, but I have to admit, we now have exponentially expanding questions. And, I still have to go two more years before I can retire, so thanks a lot!"

There was a bit of laughter, then settled back into the somber anticipation as to what in the world could come next.

"It just keeps getting better. We found, unbelievably, in the usual meticulous Luftwaffe records archives the gun camera footage from that totally destroyed FW in 1944. No one could explain how it survived the crash and fire, but there it is. How about that for a break! It clearly shows the 'Gypsy Mother' and Linda in the co-pilot seat!"

As the day progressed, it seemed that each report not just added to and confirmed the previous one, but topped it as if each succeeding presenter was obligated to out-do his predecessor. Mac got up and introduced the next speaker, the owner of Fantasy Flights, Mr. Klaus Weiss. He approached the hot-seat area this time so he could see everybody.

"I thank you all for your warm greeting. I must tell you now that we were destined to meet here, who knows how long ago, only God knows. What I am about to tell you, I have been waiting to do so most of my life. Having watched you and listened to you while we are receiving this incredible information, I know that my wait is justified!"

He moved around the room, personally greeting each one. It was such a warm, personal introduction that everyone had the same comfortable response; 'I've known you all my life!'. When he got to Rick, he looked intently into Rick's eyes and said,

"You were chosen specifically for this, you know."

Rick was immobile. He could only nod slightly and would later recall that his mouth was open as if to respond, but nothing would come forth. Klaus then stopped in front of Linda and, with a two-handed hand shake,

"At last, I have the honor and privilege of meeting the 'Edel Luftmadchen'!"

While still holding her hand, he smiled and said,

"60 years and three days ago, you shot my father's aircraft down!"

Linda unconsciously jerked her hand back in shock! Then, recovering, she reached out to him again.

"That was your father? Oh, I'm so sorry. We . . . ."

"No, please let me go on. I have thought of this moment for quite some time but I did not hope to cause any alarm with you, especially. You were somewhat of a hero of Wagnerian stature in my father's estimation all his life, and, by the way, he lived a full life, just dying in 1988. This is all so overpowering that I had hoped for a bit of levity in saying what I did, and it probably would have been taken as such had you known more of the background. Anyway, I do apologize for making you feel uncomfortable and it is such a pleasure to meet you finally. I am most anxious to tell you my part of this journey.

My father, though surviving the war, never was able to recover from the events of that day. It did change his life, which was a good thing I will now relate. For now, please allow me to read the report my father filed with the Luftwaffe for that day.

'I was returning from patrol of my sector of our region. There had been no activity anywhere in the region. I was at about 2.1Km just north of Calais when I saw a lone B-17 below and to my left at about 1.5Km. It seemed to emerge from a cloud, the only cloud in the sky at the time. Ground control called me to alert me as it had just come up on the radar. I verified it, quickly checked around for other aircraft noting that a lone B-17 with no escort was most unusual. It couldn't have been a straggler since there was no activity in the area. I immediately attacked, diving with the sun at my back, hoping for surprise. (He told me exterior to this report that attacking the heavily armed B-17 did little to promote longevity!) As I closed, I noted the strange markings, no known unit designation. Preparing to fire, I noticed that there were no gunners at any station. I was surprised and somewhat confused, but did manage to get off a two-second burst that hit the right wing as I passed down off the right side. I noticed that there was a small woman, alone in the cockpit, in the co-pilot seat. This I could not comprehend. As I drew no fire on my initial pass, I wanted to further investigate this situation. I came up and banked around level from the right side to get a closer look. I now saw another person in the cockpit in the pilot seat, but no one else at any of the gun positions. Being totally distracted, I was caught off guard. The top turret and the right waist guns began firing on me, but I still saw no gunners. I banked hard around level to avoid the stream of bullets, but I had already taken a critical hit. My aircraft was on fire and going down. I managed to get out of it and opened my parachute. I watched the B-17 heading out over the channel for a while, then it was engulfed in a cloud, the same kind I noticed when first seeing the plane. I was then trying to land safely and didn't see it again. It had just disappeared.'

"Father told me later that ground control confirmed that they had lost contact just as he had seen them vanish. Their report verified contact for just over 4 minutes, naturally claiming that he had shot it down, which he knew he had not inflicted nearly enough damage to do that, especially on the rugged B-17."

After a long pause, he added,

"Can anyone explain this? I can tell you, no one but God!"

He then told them that this was his favorite part of the story, to talk abut his father.

"My father, Herr Kurt Weiss, was an atheist most of his young life. He had experienced the aftermath of the first world war and saw Germany stripped, physically and spiritually, so he was ready and eager to grab for the hope of the 'New World Order'. Immersing himself in it left no room for God and faith. His faith consisted of what he could see and use for the moment and what could be built on for the future. My mother, on the other hand, was a good Christian woman who never gave up on him, and it was a struggle from the beginning of their relationship after her family warned her repeatedly about marrying a non-believer. Evidently, she could see something in him that nobody else saw. She prayed all her life that he would somehow be led to the Light before it was too late for him. She, in the end, was able to see her prayers answered and I thank God for the influence she had on his life at a time when he didn't even realize it."

"This was an event that changed my father's life completely. He reviewed and analyzed what had happened so many times. The evidence of it all was so overwhelming that he finally had to admit to himself that not only was God real, but that He was unquestionably with him that day. This, he told me, was not in his report to the Luftwaffe. He told me that as he approached the B-17 again, he was concentrating on the brave woman in the co-pilot seat who seemed to be taking his picture! He was without question, baffled by all this. Before he could respond in any way, the top turret and waist guns began firing at him directly. He said he distinctly remembered saying, 'Mein Gott, Helfe Mir!'. They do say there are no atheists in foxholes. Maybe so! He felt strongly that he was more than just lucky to have gotten out unharmed and also that the reason was because God had heard his plea and answered him. I don't know how he arrived at this, but he told me that one day that event would be revisited and there would be much more to verify all he had told me. He would say no more about it, but assured me that I would easily recognize it when I heard about it."

"After the war he continued to study, meditate, pray and talk to anyone with whom he felt may have a link to God. He said he knew God had spared him that day for some reason and after he had studied the Word, he concluded that it was so he could be a witness for His Glory and Compassion. He consequently did study and become a minister and was totally committed to the Lord and His Work for the rest of his life. My mother was the happiest woman around and was herself, a substantial witness to the power of prayer."

"As I said, my father somehow knew that this would happen one day and as soon as I was old enough to fully understand, he told me I would be a part of it and needed to prepare. He even mentioned a business similar to this. As you may imagine, at first the thought of doing this was highly distasteful to me, having vivid memories of what all the damage war in general and this plane in particular had done to my country and people I knew. But, as you are all aware, when God has a plan for you, He has His Way of showing you the error of your way of thinking. I can't tell you how often I went against this by trying to devote my life to music first, which failed miserably, then teaching languages, again to no avail, eventually to engineering, which led me to aeronautics, which tracked me right to where He wanted me in the first place. Can we not all acknowledge this?"

Everybody in the room answered a resounding AMEN!

"Doing it our way and falling flat until we decided maybe He has a better way! We do tend to make it hard on ourselves when we try to be so self-sufficient! Finally, with His Guidance through my earthly father and His Guiding Hand, I was made aware that this whole thing would manifest itself as a witness of God's Glory. I was 'told' that it would happen when the time was right, as is always the case with God. This one event, covering years, miles and so many people, will affect all who hear of it and it cannot be explained away. What a conversion story! There is no way to accurately assess how many lives my father may have touched for God because of this wonderous miracle and that is just his part of it . . . . imagine what our part has the potential to do!"

There was such a long period of silence the transcriber even shut down the recorder.

Chapter VII

Witnesses

Col Boggs finally got up and started his report.

We, of course, interviewed each member of the crew individually, with the exception of Rick and Linda. You will all have transcripts of this hearing if you desire."

An immediate burst of laughter covered him, as if anyone would NOT want a copy of this!

"And these interviews will be included. You will notice immediately that it appears we took one interview and copied it seven times. They are almost identical, to the letter. I would ask, for this record, that one of you folks volunteer to tell the rest what happened to you."

Sue Foster stood up and said she had never been accused of being without words. Bob quickly offered, 'Amen to that!'. When the laughter subsided, she said,

"We are so thrilled to be a part of all of this and I am sure we have what Kurt had spoken of to Klaus about the confirmation! While we were out, we were REALLY out. All of us were experiencing what I can only describe as an 'out-of-body' event. It has come to my mind that we were in a multi-dimensional effect and believe me when I tell you, it HAD to come to me. I can't even spell 'multi-dimensional'. We were completely aware of what was happening in the Gypsy as well as the FW190. We all witnessed the initial attack and saw our 'Edel' flying the Gypsy like seasoned veteran. We were witnesses to the crew firing the top turret and right waist guns at the surprised Kurt. We did hear him exclaim in German, 'My God, help me!', What he didn't tell you Klaus, was that the bullets completely riddled his cockpit panel and totally destroyed his seat back. There was no way those bullets could have missed him! Yet, he was able to get out of that burning plane, open his parachute and land safely, without so much as a scratch! He must have known at that moment that God had truly heard his plea and answered his and all of his wife's prayers as well. No wasted motion for our Lord! I think that this is also unanimous among us, that being we haven't talked abut it among ourselves, but we were only in that state, being out of our bodies, from first coming out of that nacre cloud—I've always wanted to use 'nacre' only having seen it before on crossword puzzles—to the time when we re-entered it after Kurt's plane went down."

All the others confirmed that.

"I think our primary purpose, or rather function was to be independent witnesses to these events and being incapacitated and isolated as we were, there was no way we could have gotten together and cooked this story up."

Another extended period of silence.

"I know it seems that we just keep pulling another rabbit out of the hat, so to speak, but, well, Rick and Linda, I want you to take a look at this old partial picture; all that remained of a permanent record file that was destroyed by fire. Col. Boggs handed them the photo remnant.

"Look at this Linda! The nose art is showing that it is the original Gypsy Moth! Do you recognize the one crew member still visible there?"

"That is your uncle Ned! Just as I saw him at that waist gun position!"

"No question about it, we've still got some old home movies that were taken of him when he was just a bit younger that this. That is him!"

All the others agreed that he was the one they had seen at the waist gun, firing.

"Imagine. He was in the Gypsy Moth!"

"Well, guys and gals, here's another rabbit—so were you! We were able to trace the air frame numbers back through the salvage process, which I might add made me envious of the highly organized Luftwaffe system, and were able to confirm that this Gypsy for the most part, is the original Gypsy Moth! I am sorry to say, at least to this point that we are unable to determine the identity of the rest of the crew, but we're working on it. One other fragment from that file read 'NSSEN', maybe a part of a name or nothing but we are still at it. If not for your video, we wouldn't have known this match with your uncle existed. The photo remnant was filed in 'Misc. England, 1944". If that tells you what a haystack this needle was in. We also believe your voice was that crew commander but to this point, we cannot identify him either. I do apologize for that. Seems the more we get into these old records, it was hard to remember that we won! We must believe after witnessing that landing that he was a B-17 Aircraft Commander."

With all due respect to you, Mac, he still is this aircraft commander!"

"Couldn't agree with you more, Rick. In my years of flying a B-17 I have seldom landed as smoothly as youall did, so I would say your 'instructor' was, or is, the best!"

"Okay, so what are we going to do with all of this? One thing for sure, Klaus. When word of this gets out, you're gonna have to find some more B-17's!"

Klaus spoke again,

"Please forgive me if I revert to my heritage in what I will say next, but I know no other way. This is not the time to be humble! Jesus taught us to have a humble heart and, as you say, to take a back seat in most situations, but He had his moments. Mein Herren und Damen, it is time to drive the money changers out of the temple!"

Instant cheers and applause!

"Linda, I think we have just received our marching orders."

"Yeah, and I also think everybody is up for the fight!"

"I am certainly no prophet and claim no insight superior to any of you, but see if this makes any logical sense out of my reasoning to you all . . ."

"YOUALL! Klaus, are you from south Germany?"

Much laughter . . .

"No, but I did spend a while in Marietta, Georgia."

"That's it, then."

"And, Rick, thank you for the break . . . I tend to get carried away with this, so I appreciate the 'brake' on my enthusiasm. It has been on my mind so long, now that the lid is off, it is difficult to suppress it."

"As I iterated, my father had some insight into all of this and told me as many times as I asked that this event would occur when the time was right—God's time. We are all aware of the continuing decline in both numbers and activity among Christians world wide, from all and I DO mean ALL quarters. We are told that the enemy will not prevail against the Church, the Body of Christ, so I am of the opinion that this is a marshaling order for the counter attack. Without being flamboyant, He has given a sign that He is alive and in charge, but the acceptance of this is still as He deems it, everyone's free will choice. As in everything else from Him, this will require faith from those to whom we have the duty now to witness! I also believe that it is exactly what it is; our duty. In that respect, we are in the same situation the Apostles were 2000 years ago. You must all realize how extremely blessed we are to have been chosen to be an active part of this."

"Rick is the numerologist in the family, but I do think it is significant that there are twelve of us involved in this experience. That number seemed to serve Jesus adequately."

"From what I have observed and sensed being with you remarkable people, I know now that the inspiration was well-founded for my following suggestion. I have given this much thought followed by much prayer followed by close listening. What I hear is an approval to proceed; I propose that the special relationship with this crew and this aircraft be made a more permanent one to serve as a ministerial team. Since you didn't get your 'mission' in on your flight, I offer you a new mission. Your target is the most despicable enemy the world has ever known and you are in a most enviable position to use your recent experience to deliver a significant blow against him. If you are of the one mind, and I believe you are, let us develop further what our Lord has led us to, a 'gypsy-like' wandering ministry, a hangar revival! We are truly at war and the stakes have never been higher. This is a battle for the hearts and souls, no greed for riches or territory. It is further my opinion that once this story is officially made public, funding for such an operation will not be a problem. As to the technicalities of putting such together, we have contacts within this room that can help make this happen and expeditiously. What do you say?"

Rick was on his feet.

"If you are asking if we want to live the dream of a lifetime and serve the Lord in doing that, I'll have to think about that some . . . okay, you talked me into it, you silver-tongued rascal!"

He looked at Linda, who was laughing and nodding enthusiastically.

"This is something that fits better than anything in that movie line, 'He has given us a deal we can't refuse!'"

All the others chimed in with equal enthusiasm.

"We are IN!"

"Mac, you have yourself a crew!"

:And a finer one I couldn't even hope for!"

Again there was much hugging, hand-shaking and laughing. Bill Fisher said that they can all be assured that this room had never experienced anywhere near this level of joy and it was a delight to see.

"Klaus, is it possible for Gypsy to stay here at Foster, sort of being based here?"

"Rick, it is not only possible but the deal is done. You see, I was so sure of this outcome I have already arranged for hangar space for Gypsy and office space as well."

"Well, all I can say about this is that it refutes that tired old saw 'if it sounds too good to be true, it probably is'. In this case, if it sounds too good to be true, then it must be from God! Can you guys believe this? We are a crew on a B-17!!! Thank you, Jesus for this incredible blessing! Lets go see our plane!"

Col. Boggs added, "We have to determine if the battle damage is in any way detrimental to the flight characteristics of Gypsy. If not, I think it would be a beneficial part of the witness from her part! We did notice the right wing dip slightly on your landing, possibly some lift lost on that wing on flare-out but, we will check it out. Either way, we will make arrangements for it to stay right there at Foster Field even if repairs are needed."

"Mac, would you and Chuck teach me to fly Gypsy?"

"Yeah, you might be trainable. I didn't witness that turn of yours, but I did see a recording of the ground track radar. Maybe we can do something about that fifteen mile 180 you made!"

Everybody in the room enjoyed that!

"Well, laugh if you must, but it wasn't just me, you know. It was just hard for an old seasoned war bird like Gypsy to quit and turn off a bombing run."

"Well said! That'll get you lessons!"

"Linda, you can forget any birthday or Christmas gifts for me from now on! I have you and Gypsy, both blessings from God, and no one could ask for more!"

"Okay, I'll sure remind you of that and, thank you for listing me first!"

Klaus told them that they will be contacted individually for more specific details on their input to all of this as soon as they have had a chance to digest and contemplate the possibilities of what opportunities lie ahead.

"I ask you for your ideas as this is nothing close to finalized without your consultation. I am only certain that it will be done! May God bless you and send His angels to guard your hearts."

It would almost take the threat of calling in a SWAT team to get everyone to finally leave the building. There was so much enthusiasm, so many great ideas already springing up. It was evident that these 'seeds' had indeed fallen on fertile ground!

The trip home for Rick and Linda consisted of Rick babbling and Linda nodding.

"Wait 'til the kids hear we have our own B-17! Did you hear Ken say that he still has contacts in the clothing business that would get us all flight suits when we decided on patch designs and all? Can you believe all of this is happening to us?"

"Rick, pull over!"

"Why"

"I'm going to drive the rest of the way home."

"Why?"

"Well, you're going to be locked in the trunk!"

"Okay, I get your subtle hint, but please show a little respect to a future B-17 pilot!"

"Okay, if you will show a little respect in return for a future crazy person!"

When they got home and settled in, Linda called their friends.

"Phil, you both need to be here to help me dispose of Rick's body. I'm about to tape his mouth shut and when that happens, I know he will explode!"

"Kinda wound up, is he?"

"Understatement!"

"It must have been a great meeting. We'll see you shortly."

"Linda, I need to be sure I thank you right now for your love and patience that allowed me to be in this position to receive God's incredible blessing! I know I don't say it as often as I should, but you will know that the thanksgiving is always on my mind. Thank God for sending me your way!"

"I'm just glad we finally got to where He can show us what He has had planned for us all this time. This is going to be good."

Phil and Edith came in prepared to be the recipient of Rick's eagerness.

"Listen to this. Klaus suggested that first, the Gypsy be kept here at Foster Field as home base, but then, he added that this adventure of ours was just to get us in place to use it as a springboard for a unique ministry! He visualizes us traveling in Gypsy and telling our story in person with, of course, other speakers, all of us spreading the Word for the Glory of God. What do you think about that?"

They both looked at each other and smiled.

"You listen to this! We talked about that very thing last night, I mean down to the inclusion of the plane being kept here, the whole thing! I'm not even going to say 'can you believe it'. Here lately, those are wasted words."

"You know, you two are in on this up to your necks, starting with your visualizing Linda and I flying that plane and now this! You have obviously been invited to join our happy little band!"

"Klaus figures without anything but instinct to back it up, that the funding will be the least obstacle. He thinks also that we'll have sponsors running over each other to get in on this, maybe even a movie! Anyway, it is in God's Capable Hands!"

"I thank you for including Phil and I in this for whatever reason. We all know that it is by Design, so there is no question for the purpose. We are just anxious to do whatever we can. One thing, we have to consider, we're going to have lots of flak when this is made public. As much as is going on with any mention of Christianity in any public place, and all the pure hate being spread, the enemy has made it known that he isn't going to let it develop without a fight . . ."

"Flak, how appropriate! I agree, Edith. That just confirms that we are at war, so we can expect a powerful fight. One thing, though, we know that our side will win, but it is our duty to make sure we get all we can to come to our Leader"

Rick went to answer the phone,

"Yes Klaus, we are discussing it all right now with some friends . . . . I almost said it again, 'I don't believe it' . . . . Klaus, that is wonderful news! . . . . Yes, we do need to get that office set up as soon as possible so they can have contact info . . . . no, I agree . . . we shouldn't jump in until we have the plan set but we do need to press."

"Thank you, Klaus. We will all meet tomorrow. That is such good news! Yes, we will talk to you then."

"Wow! This is taking off, so to speak. Klaus has been contacted by 'MY ANGEL', a Christian mission organization that has a monthly publication, "Know News is Good News' with a worldwide readership presently of 35 million readers plus. They want to run our story and then do monthly reports of our activity! Klaus said they were most generous with their offer, even after he refused exclusivity. He told them what we have done so far or will do is for God's whole world so we cannot be limited in any way."

"You know, I like that guy more all the time and I haven't even met him!"

"Oh, you will! What we need to do is get on that office setup. We have to be available for contact. So much to be doing, yet I feel like it is almost being done for us! Can you two meet with us tomorrow?"

"We sure can! We wouldn't miss out on this for anything!"

"I have got to check on Mrs. Johnson. Can't forget our new charge. She is surely home by now. She had said that the hospital insisted on bringing her home, I imagine for their own after-care to make sure she was adequately housed and all. I had offered, but you know, I think she really kinda liked the thought of riding in that ambulance, especially since she was sitting up this time.""Yeah, she is there. We did call and check just before we came over here. We took the liberty of telling her we would all drop by a bit later."

"Great! I feel so good about how everything is going, I just don't want to slight anybody, especially her. We can go down there anytime you want. Rick, got your ransom?"

"You have to know that Captain now has two 'marks'."

"Phil, you too?"

"Well, he is so nice about it."

They all went down to Mrs. Johnson's house that commanded the intersection. Captain was in the back yard when they arrived, not expecting them at this time, but he quickly flew into his door in the back porch. He could be heard yelping, not barking. Rick was certain that he was telling them that his 'mother' was home.

Mrs. Johnson met them at the door.

"Well, look at you! You're moving around very well!"

"Yes, and please do come in. I am so glad to see youall. I do feel fine now. Coming home does help a lot. My Captain is so glad to see me. I hope he wasn't trouble for you and again, I do appreciate so much you looking after things for me. You must be Phil and Edith."

"Yes ma'am, good to meet you in person."

"God has blessed me yet again with His Own."

"Thank you, Mrs. Johnson."

"Please call me Martha. Won't you please come in and have some coffee."

"Yes, thank you. That will be nice, Mrs., uh, Martha."

She showed them into the den and Linda went with her to the kitchen to start the coffee.

"Well, since I've been out of touch, what has been going on. Anything exciting?"

They smiled remembering that she had no idea as to what had happened to Rick and Linda the past few days.

"It's been different Mrs., uh, Martha."

"Good! Don't any of you ever let life get bland. The Lord intended for us to live fully by not just seeing, but experiencing all He has given us here on earth. I believe our heaven starts right here!"

"You have four that feel the same way. I want to apologize again for us not being good Christians and neighbors by not getting around to checking in with you sooner. We correct that starting today!"

"Oh, that's all right. I know how busy lives can get. My Artie and I were always on the dead run, trying to make up for the time we were apart during the war. I think we did a pretty good job of it, too. Youall would have liked Artie. He was so full of life. People used to kid us about him being the comedian, Artie Johnson, which he didn't mind at all. He liked anyone who made people laugh. Said there was too much sorrow in this world. Of course, our name is pronounced 'Johnson', but is spelled 'Johnssen'"

"Do you have a picture of him?"

"Oh my, yes! Here is my favorite one of him as a dashing Captain in the Army Air Corp. Here he is, my Artie!"

She showed them the picture of a young Army Captain in uniform wearing pilot wings.

"He was a pilot?"

"Yes, he flew the B-17. Are you familiar with them?"

"Well, we have just recently been introduced personally to one in particular. Wait a minute . . . did you say your name was spelled 'Johnssen'?"

"Yes, that is correct. Unusual spelling, isn't it?"

"Mrs Johnssen, do you remember the name of your husband's aircraft?"

"Well, I should hope so. To forget that would be like forgetting my own name, which is what it was."

"Oh, then it was Martha?"

"No, here is another one that shows it."

She got a picture from the top of the desk and handed it to them.

"This is my favorite one."

They looked at the picture in stunned silence. There, clear and plain as day was the ten man crew in front of their aircraft, the 'Gypsy Moth'! Nobody could say a word.

"He said this picture held memories of the most important time of his life—the plane that he had named after me, and the men in his crew, whom he considered his 'kids'. He was a kid himself! When I was young, I loved jewelry and flashy clothes and I also loved to travel, so I was nicknamed 'Gypsy'. My mother was from Alabama and with her strong accent, when she called me, it sounded like 'Moth' since she always dropped the last 'a'. Artie picked it up when we were dating and he ever since called me his 'Gypsy Moth'."

The inscription on the picture read, 'To my Gypsy Moth, Love always, Artie'! There, right at the end of the group was Ned, Rick's uncle. Just under him was the name of the aircraft commander, Captain Arthur Johnssen.

As soon as Rick could talk, he called Ed Boggs and told him that the mystery of the 'NSSEN' was solved and that the A/C was positively identified as Captain Arthur Johnssen. He then came to Mrs. Johnssen, took her hand and said,

"Mrs., uh, Martha, please have a comfortable seat. Do we have a story to tell you!"

Chapter VIII

Attack Formation

Rick and Linda proceeded to tell Martha the whole story of their incredible encounter, from beginning to present. They both realized that in doing this, they were getting some good practice for the upcoming ministry presentations they would all be making Since they felt it was 'from God', that made it even more necessary to be as accurate as possible.

When they had updated the information, the silence of contemplation was lengthy, finally broken by Martha.

"I thank you so much for sharing this with me. It makes me even more proud of my Artie to hear that God used him to get youall down safely.

This was not his first time to work with the Lord in that capacity though. He had told me over the years about several times when he knew God was there with them, holding poor shot-up Gypsy Moth together until they could land. You know, I have wondered for years why the Lord has left me here when He knew how much I wanted to go home to be with Him and see my Artie again. Now I know and, as usual, ask His forgiveness for ever questioning His Will for me. He always has a plan for us and it's always better than what we could ever hope to come up with."

"Martha, I believe I can speak for us all when I say that we are so happy to have you as a part of this adventure and welcome you to the ministry!"

Everyone quickly agreed and each gave her a hug.

"You're going to make quite an addition. Can't wait for the others to meet you."

"After all you wonderful friends have done for me, I am almost ashamed to ask for more . . . I can hear my mother now, 'Mahth! Ladies don't impose!' . . . so please forgive me if I ask if I can meet them soon and see the Gypsy Moth."

"Mrs., uh, Martha, you just name it. As soon as you are up to it, it will be an honor to go with you!"

"That is so nice of youall. Could we possibly go tomorrow?"

"We'll go in the morning, say around 8 am, if that sounds okay."

"Yes it does and I'll be ready for sure."

"We'll bring Captain too, or we'll have to endure that sad scowl when we leave."

"He will love that. He enjoys going places. He always did like to travel. Must have been influenced by my gypsy life."

As soon as they got home they called the crew and related the 'Martha' story. The response from each was the same . . . silence then laughter and 'what next'!

The next morning they met Phil and Edith at Martha's house. They had gone down to check on her to see if they could help her get ready. She met them at the door, ready to go.

They got everyone loaded and in the process were subjected to their benevolence toward Captain being rewarded by a lick on the hand. That could have possibly been prompted also by the fact that Rick had a piece of chocolate in his hand.

"Martha, the whole crew will be there today. They all want to meet you and welcome you to the group."

"This is so exciting! It is such a blessing for an old lady like me to feel that the Spirit sees fit to work in my life! One of my favorite scriptures is 2 Corinthians 4:16 and I do feel that, even though I am wasting away outwardly, inwardly I now truly feel that I am being renewed daily."

"Martha, you are becoming a very bright light in this ministry."

The trip to the field was shortened by Martha telling so many stories that Artie had told her, one after the other confirming that God's Hand was in his crew's protection. He even told about his waist gunner, Moe, as he was known to the crew, and Ned to his nephew, Rick, having the Gypsy drop instantly as a flak round exploded just outside his station. A piece of flak 'parted his hair' and buried into the metal overhead. I the 'air pocket' had not caused that quick drop, he was certain that flak would have hit him right between the eyes. Rick had heard that same story from the source and saw the piece of flak Ned had dug out of the frame when they had landed.

They went into the hangar and found everyone already there, some in the office, some in the hangar discussing the physical set-up for the revival. There in the center of it all was the Gypsy Moth, now with her 'new' old name back. The story about that name was still so incredible, having the Fantasy Company arrive at it from a totally different reason, but coming up with the original. It would have been quite a coincidence if there was such!

It was almost as if the aircraft knew she would be shown off to a V.I.P.

She shined and just emitted a glow that seemed to say 'got to look my best for my Mom!'

Martha was almost overwhelmed by the sight of this beauty that shared her name and that had been such an important part of her partner's life. The memories rushed back as she stood there and let them flow over her. As tears rolled down her cheeks, Captain, previously grafted to her side, alerted. He looked up at Martha, whined and barked once. He then went toward the Gypsy, stopped and looked back at Martha as if to say, 'come on'! They walked around to the side door and helped Martha up into it. Captain waited for her to get in then he jumped up beside her. Then as if responding to a command, his ears went up, he cocked his head slightly and went up immediately to the flight deck. There was a whimper again, then he put his front paws on the left seat and eased his head down as if it were in someone's lap. Martha had moved up there by now and put her hand on captain's head.

"I feel him, too, boy. Artie, I know you can hear me and as you can see, I am in the best of hands here. This is so wonderful to be so close to you. I know now why I am still here, so I will do all I can here, then I will be home whenever He decides I have finished what He wanted me to do. Thank you, Lord Jesus for allowing me this blessing. You just lead and I will follow!"

Captain then got out of the seat and they got Martha into it.

"It is so hard to believe that I am sitting in this place where my Artie flew through so many terrible missions."

She sat there for a while in deep thought then turned to Rick,

"We've got a lot to do, so let's get at it! I've had so many blessings all through my life and this is sure to be one of the greatest so I'm anxious to get into it!"

They got outside again and as they walked away from Gypsy, Captain alerted again, looked up at the flight deck, barked once then went immediately to Martha's side.

"Linda, look at that! Are we into something good or what! This whole place is alive with the Spirit"

The rest of the crew came and met Martha and she was so happy to see and meet them all. She radiated with each handshake, hug and word of welcome from each of them. Captain was right by her side, checking them, then approving each one as they rubbed his head.

They all migrated into the classroom as they chatted away about what may be just ahead for them and what a wonderful opportunity it was for them to serve.

When there was a temporary lull in the conversation, Allen went up to the front.

"This is a good time to get started on some of the common items that face all of us, so that we may be on the same page when asked about these things. Charlotte and I have already been approached about the 'Godliness' of having spirits of the deceased involved with our lives. Have any of you run across that yet?"

"Ken and I were asked about that very thing!"

"How did you answer it?"

"The words came out without hesitation. In the first place, we didn't 'call up the deceased' as it was described. The Lord sent His helpers to us Himself. He has throughout history used angels, demons, spirits and even animals in many ways to accomplish His tasks. We didn't hear a comment after we finished by telling them we were sorry that their god was so restricted and maybe they should consider ours, Who is capable of doing anything anytime with anyone He chooses to do His bidding."

"Bravo! We all need to keep that 'hidden in our hearts' for future use! The opportunities will surely come. Linda and I had that very same talk after the flight and we came to the same conclusion as yours. We couldn't imagine limiting God because of man's interpretation.

I guess great minds just run together!"

"Yeah, especially if they are in Christ!"

The phone in the office adjacent to the classroom rang.

"Our first call!"

Chuck was closest so he got the call as Martha started to speak,

"I was just looking at youall and you positively glow! Please forgive me as I know I'm repeating myself, but this is so wonderful! Just a week ago I was puttering around the house wondering why I was still here and all of a sudden, I already find myself asking for just a little more time to see what I can get done for the Lord with you, His Own. Besides being with my Artie, this is my greatest blessing by far."

Chuck came in beaming.

"Well crew, we are officially in business. That was Dr. Graham Williams himself! He had received our story and wanted to know if we could use an old evangelist in one of our presentations! Can you imagine that? Someone like him! Well, there's no one like him. Anyway, he laughed when he said that we should book him pretty soon because he felt his 'sand was running out'. He said he had retired from the revival circuit, but he was so impressed with our story he wanted to be a part of getting it going."

"Wow! Graham Williams! Yes, children, we are definitely open! We have to call Klaus. He will be elated."

"I told Dr. Williams that Klaus would confirm time and such with him very soon."

Ken brought out a picture he had gotten and enlarged.

"How do you like this?"

It was a sky blue flight suit and had a patch on the shoulder with a shield, the shield of faith, with a sword on it. He said the design had been inspired by a Psalm he recalled, 'With the praise of God in their mouth and a two-edged sword in their hands', the two-edged sword being the Word of God. On the hilt of the sword on either edge were the symbols for Alpha and Omega.

"Well, what do you think?"

"Ken, it is perfect!!"

"Yeah, when can we get those?"

Everybody was so excited about them. They all knew he had mentioned the flight suits, but no one realized he had gone into the design work so soon.

"Youall will all look so good in those uniforms."

"Martha, 'youall' includes you, too!"

"Oh, no, don't waste that on this old lady."

"Ma'am, you are one of us and that includes everything we get, have or do!"

"Yes, and with all due respect, we won't take no for an answer!"

Oh, my goodness! I'm going to cry again."

"Look at this! We can even get Captain a suit, too!"

"Anybody have any changes or additions for this?"

"No, I think we are all so thankful for this, you had some inspiration for it and it is so perfect, no one would or could top it!"

"Thank you, Ken. The only addition I can think of is a design for our group patch for the back of the jackets. I will see what I can come up with for that. That patch can be added anytime later whenever we decide what we are to be called."

"Great! We'll get them sized and they will have them finished and delivered in seven days, how about that!"

"Well, it sure helps to know those who know those!

"I mentioned the jackets. Linda and I have the A-2s and I am almost afraid to ask this as I seem to already know the answer, but does anyone else have the A-2 jackets?

Everyone in the room raised their hands!

"Why am I not surprised! Good! Martha, we will get yours on the way, then we'll have the patches put on them"

"Now, mind you, it's a little large for me, but I do have Artie's jacket. Will that be okay?"

"You still have his A-2 leather jacket?"

Yes, he had it completely renovated several years ago and it is still in original condition."

"Yes Ma'am, that one will be just fine!"

Everyone was just looking at each other and shaking their heads in awe.

"Guess we might just as well get used to this sort of thing. It seems like this is how our lives are going to be from now on."

Mac came in with a fax he had just received from Klaus.

"He sent a preliminary outline with the resources available to us for the presentation. He wants it made perfectly clear that this is only a guide. The program details are yours."

"Hey, this pretty well covers what we had been talking about. What do you think?

The video they could have for the big screen projection would cover the video Linda had taken, the Luftwaffe gun camera footage from Kurt's FW-190, ground control radar track recording and, of course, the battle damage and spent shell casings. His suggestion was that each couple would take a segment and describe what was being shown, then Martha would be introduced at the last of the presentation to add her participation. Klaus would then introduce the guest evangelist who would speak about what these events seemed to say and how they related to God's Word.

Everyone was well pleased with the format and began to talk about who would do what. Rick and Linda would explain her video, Mac and Chuck would present their facts about the guns being plugged and inoperable, and the radio being out of service, then show the shell casings from Gypsy with the Air Force reports on their analyses. Ken and Marianne took the Luftwaffe records of Kurt's attack and Kurt's description of the guns firing at him, Allen and Charlotte would relate Kurt's attack with the still-evident battle damage with the time factor being stressed. Bob and Sue would continue with the time sequence by documenting the Richter Radar complex shown in Linda's video with post-strike photos of the 8th Air Force showing its total destruction the day after this flight. Martha would tell of Artie's personal spiritual faith and how he had felt so often God's protection of him and his crew in getting the Gypsy home. Klaus would be the coordinator of it all and would fill in Kurt's life after the attack. Phil and Edith would lend support to it all with their dream visions of the flight.

It was coming together and it was a good fit! They were relaxing in the class-room talking about how well it was going when Captain stood with ears straight up. 'He didn't bark but actually leaned against Martha's leg. A man walked in and went straight to Captain and reached down and touched his head. Captain whined once, licked his hand and lay down at Martha's feet again.

"Hi, can we help you?"

"I've got some projection and sound equipment to deliver to this hangar. Where would you like it?"

"Projection equipment . . . it must be from Klaus . . . yes, please bring it in. You can bring the truck right in to the maintenance cage over there and we'll put it in there for now."

"Be right back. Hey, that is a beautiful B-17!"

"Yeah, we're kinda partial to it."

The phone rang in the office again and Charlotte went to answer it.

'Air Ministry, how can we help you? . . . yes . . . who? . . . well, sure . . . we're all here now, so it is a great time to come ahead. Thank you and God bless you, too.' "Guys, I don't know what is happening but somebody is really shining on us. An anonymous donor has ordered 5,000 chairs and they are on the way out!"

"Anonymous donor? Praise God from Whom all blessings flow! That is wonderful!"

"Charlotte, I think you have just named us! Air Ministry! How does everybody like that?"

"That is just the ticket! Perfect!"

"It's us!"

"Great! Air Ministry it is then. That is the name we will put on our cards."

"Yeah, and we need to put the double edged sword insignia on it also."

"Done!"

"We are really going now!"

"Then, that is the name for our patch. Now I will get the design drawn up with that included!"

Ken laughed saying we would need to be careful in the UK or they will think we are from the government. He was by the phone so it was his turn to answer. He came out of the office saying it was Klaus.

"That was Klaus. I answered 'Air Ministry' and there was silence for a moment, then he burst out, 'Du Liebe Gott! I like that name!' I told him we did too, then told him about the deliveries of the equipment and the chairs . . . he had nothing to do with any of it! He did call Dr. Williams after Mac had contacted him about the offer to speak at our first revival. Guys, he scheduled Dr. Williams and our first meeting in two weeks!!!"

"Two Weeks!!! What if we hadn't gotten that equipment or chairs?"

"I asked that same question. He told me to look again at the deliveries and remember 'for whom we are working'!"

When the phone rang again, they were almost afraid to answer it. Linda went this time.

'Air Ministry, how may we help you? Hi, this is Linda . . . yes . . . of course I know you. So nice to speak to you. Yes, we have just confirmed our first meeting, which will be two weeks from Friday here at our base. No, we can't, or rather won't do anything exclusive as our Lord certainly doesn't exclude any of us. You may confirm this time with Mr. Klaus Weiss but as far as we are concerned here, we'll welcome the coverage.

Oh, well, if you have already talked to him and he sent you to us, by all means plan on it and we will look forward to seeing you then. Thank you and God Bless you!'

"Folks that was Cathy Norwood from All Christian Network. They want to televise our program!"

Everybody cheered and praised God. Captain barked along with the cheering.

"Look at the events that have occurred this blessed day! It is more than I can comprehend! We have not hit a lick at a snake and all these blessings have fallen on us! We are catching His full Grace so now we have to do our part. You know, we do need to be prepared for the 'flak' that will surely come at us now that we have put the enemy on notice that we are for real and are after him. We are definitely showing up on his radar now."

Chapter IX

Maximum Effort

The two weeks that seemed such a short preparation time at first proved to be even shorter in the experiencing of them! That time had passed before the crew could believe it.

"Here we are folks. It's time to spread the Word!"

"As fast as this time has gone, I still think we got the most of it, thanks to all of those who have helped so much and, of course, thanks to God."

Rick had drawn up a patch design which he knew was inspired. He could not take credit for it especially after he reviewed the significance of it, which he was asked about. It was certainly more than just the three bladed prop design for the B-17.

"Oh, don't get him started! We'll have to send out for pizza!"

"Well, since you asked, yes, there is a bit of symbolism in this design. The obvious three-bladed prop is the Trinity. Each blade is made up of four triangles, totaling twelve, for the apostles. Numerically . . ."

"Oh, here we go!"

"As I said, numerically speaking, nine is significant in my life and is evidently so in the Bible. I'm not well-versed in numerology but can't help but notice thee recurring 'coincidences' in God's world. I believe

He has something to say to us, in numbers as well as words. Now, our number system is based on 0-9. In the triangle of each blade in the design, there are 180 degrees each. Reducing that to it's lowest number, it is 9. Note that the blades are 120 degrees apart, 3 times 120 = 360 = 9. Also, there are 72 degrees between the points of a drawing of a star, 7+2=9. Biblically, 72 disciples, 144,000, 153 fish, just to name a few. There were 9 generations from Adam to Noah and 9 from Noah to Abraham. Abraham was 99 when he received God's Covenant. The numerologists say that 9 is a complete cycle of growth and that a '9' person whose birthday equals 9, as mine, 4/30/1937 = 27=9, that person's true mission is to serve as a minister of God. Since Linda is a 9 as well, I'd say we've found our mission. Aren't you glad you asked?"

The run-through of the video went smoothly and each made their notes for their commentary. Klaus had his intros down and was anxious to get this first one going. The sound system was working well and all was ready.

Just after noon, they were setting up chairs with volunteers from all the churches in the area when they noticed a small man in a dark suit, carrying a briefcase entering the hangar. Klaus was nearby and went to greet him.

"Good afternoon, my name is Klaus Weiss. Welcome to Air Ministry. With what may we help you?"

"There is nothing you can help me with other than giving me more reasons to shut you down!"

Rick had come over to them by now.

"What? "What did you say? What are you talking about?"

Now the crew members were all gathering around.

"My name is George I. Kelroy and I am an attorney with the Civil Office of Liberties Infringement Counsel. I have read your accounts of the so-called 'Divine Intervention' during your flight. I'll tell you right up front that I believe none of this religious bunk and there is no way we will allow you to perpetrate this hoax on the public for your own personal gains. I will be here tonight to observe and note what is done. If things go as I expect them to, you will receive a restraining order come Monday."

Rick was first as they all clamored to respond,

"Mr. Kilroy,"

"That's KELroy!"

"Right, Mr. Kelroy, let me tell YOU right up front that my initial reaction to your comments was to stuff you into that trash bin over there. Most of us are well aware of the work your organization is doing in this country for the enemy, all under the guise of 'protecting the public'. Well, I'm going to show you the difference a relationship with Jesus Christ can and has made in my life. Instead of following my natural instinct to allow you to provoke me to violence, I'm going to pray that the Lord touches your heart, opens your ears and exchanges that cold hardness for the peace of His love."

The whole crew and volunteers applauded and cheered loudly.

Kelroy sputtered, started to speak, then turned and stormed out.

"I'll be back tonight!"

"I think we have crossed the enemy coastline. The flak is picking up now."

Linda told Rick she was proud of him.

"When I saw you going over there, knowing how you feel about that organization, I remembered what the old Rick would have been expected to do, so folks, you just witnessed another of the Lord's miracles!"

Again, all cheered and applauded Rick's actions.

"Can you believe that guy? His name is G.I. Kelroy! That's got to be some kind of joke someone is playing on us! Kilroy was here!!! Come on!"

Klaus spoke up when the laughter had died down,

"Yes, and I could hardly contain myself thinking about the acronym C.O.L.I.C.—all I could think of was my recollection of the definition of 'colic'—a 'severe spasmodic abdominal pain'"

The laughter shook the hangar. Captain joined in again, barking and jumping on his hind legs.

"Rick, of course, did right in reminding us of the course of action in which our Lord has instructed us. We all must pray for him and all those like him. We must not waiver and use this type of confrontation as an opportunity, not a detriment. Just recall what has happened here recently and remember that we had very little to do with any of it other than to give praise and thanks to Him from Whom all comes. As you say, there is flak, but we are protected by the 'shield of faith'! Let's proceed now and make the Lord glad He chose us!"

That encounter was just sobering enough to bring them all back to the reality that everything would not be smooth and easy as it had been. They were all aware of the potential for problems and were told to remember that the level of attack was usually indicative of the level of threat they posed to the enemy. As Klaus said when he was walking out,

"Consider it all joy!"

What it accomplished was to solidify the group as one with the common bond of resolve to give this war their best effort

Word was out and the media had been buzzing for the last two weeks. The ministry, in the interim, had received such great support from all over the world that it did inspire them. There was however some serious opposition to what they were doing; serious to the point of threats of physical violence. That is when they knew they were hitting a raw nerve. This, too, was known and there were many volunteers offering their services with security. The battle lines were forming.

Phil and Edith joined Rick and Linda as they went outside to check the crowd. Just at that time they noticed a man on the tarmac just outside the gate to the hangar area. Another man was standing over him, leaning down and appeared to be checking him out. They went over to him to see if they could help.

"Do we need to call 911?"

The man, now looking somewhat familiar to them, said that would not be necessary since he seemed to be okay, just passed out for some reason. Phil went over to the man and as he touched him, he was stopped by a firm hand on his arm.

"I will take care of him, sir, but thank you for your concern."

"Sure!"

As Phil backed away he motioned for them to follow him, which they did. When they were far enough away, they all huddled around Phil as he spoke softly,

"That man on the ground had a bomb on him! Must be something like C-4. I saw the belt and felt it!"

Rick said he thought the man was dead because he had the 'color'.

When they looked toward where the men had been, nobody was there! There was no one within 50 feet of where the bomber had been!

"Now what?"

"Rick, that was the man who brought the projection and sound equipment the other morning!"

"Yeah, you're right! And now he has stopped the bomber! Folks, I think we have just seen an angel! I say we just keep this quiet for now."

"Wow! Angels and demons! They are indeed among us!"

They went back to the hangar and noticed 'volunteers' all over, helping people find seats, handing out pamphlets and watching everything that was going on. It was already evident that this was going to be SRO! By the time Klaus went up to the dais, the hangar was full! People were everywhere!

"Ladies and gentlemen, I welcome you to the inaugural flight of the Air Ministry. We apologize for the shortage of seating, but being our first effort, we didn't know what or how many to expect. I again do apologize for your inconvenience but thank God for your presence. You are about to witness a summary of one of the most incredible events in modern times—the overt miracle of the Hand of the Living God at work."

"You will hear from the people that were blessed in being a part of this event as they narrate the video presentation. When they complete their story we have a most special guest that will speak to you. Again, thank you for being here and may our Lord bless you with this presentation.,"

Linda and Rick led off with their account of the events from the wake-up call through the fog delay, flight video and the miracle landing. At one point, Rick whispered to Linda,

"I see him! I see Kelroy!"

"Good, just speak like you are talking directly to him!"

The people were really absorbed in the presentation and clapping, gasping and praising God. Klaus introduced each couple as they went through their part and finally came to Martha. For her part, they had gotten the same crew picture she had with the original crew with Artie and some archive pictures of Gypsy after being shot practically out of the sky. She told about his faith being instrumental in knowing the Lord was with them and saved them for something. Though he didn't know it at the time, this was to be it! When she had finished her short talk, she got a standing ovation, which touched her deeply.

Klaus again got up to introduce the next speaker, Dr. Graham Williams. The reception was tremendous! The audience went wild and cheered him so that it surely was heard in town!

Graham Williams humbly thanked the enthusiastic crowd and as he always did, gave thanks to God for His Spirit being so evident in the gathering.

"I know that youall who have been around me before may find this hard to believe, but I am really at a loss for words!"

Much applause and laughter!

"I don't know how to follow the wonders we have all just experienced. Is there any doubt in anyone's mind that this whole marvelous event was the work of our Living God?"

He looked directly at Kelroy as there was a resounding 'No!' with cheering and applause from the audience.

"Praise God! Praise God! And, while praising Him, I want to apologize to Him for my part in His needing to do anything more than He has previously done to attract our attention. It is most embarrassing and humbling to remember the many blessings He heaps upon us to show His love. We take them for granted and expect and constantly ask for more. We never take the time to thank Him or ask what we can do for Him! It is always what WE want, need and must have!

Instead of throwing up His hands in disgust, He further demonstrates His message of love and forgiveness by sending us a 'memo' to the effect 'I'm still here and committed to you. I'm asking you to remember me, change your ways and return to me. Don't make me come down there!' I added that last line!

You know how He works. It's always our choice. He wants us to WANT to do His bidding because we love Him! That's all He really wants. He doesn't need for us to offer Him anything materially; He already owns it all! Except for our love. He won't demand that of us, it must be given by us freely.

He welcomes all to come to Him and tells us His yoke is easy, but we try to put His Way in our earthly context and it is too hard for many to see His eternal offer to us. We all want the blessings and treasures He has promised us but we just don't want to fool with the basics. Don't you think that the Creator of the Universe would rather handle it His way? In truth, access to this treasure is simple to obtain. We first need to believe and understand that we can do nothing without His being completely involved in our lives and love Him with all that we are. Then, follow the instructions in Matthew 6:33, 'Seek first the Kingdom of God and His Righteousness and all these things will be added unto you'. Now right here, let me make a very important point. Just reading the Scripture and going to church regularly, while highly recommended as most helpful, is not all that 'seeking' entails. Too many think that by going through the mechanics of worship they are going all out for the Lord. James 1:22 speaks volumes to that, 'Be DOERS of the Word and not hearers only, deceiving yourselves'. Therefore, if you are not living what you profess to believe, it is obvious to those around you and, most importantly, to the Lord God Almighty that you are 'deceiving yourself and your salt has lost its flavor. That is definitely NOT following the path of His Word. He is asking us to get back on that path!

I know, I know, I am rambling a bit, but folks I'm still a bit unnerved by all we just witnesses. Now I want to mention that word 'miracle' here. Miracles have been defined as 'unusual events attributed to some supernatural source. I am here to tell you, my brothers and sisters that this event imminently qualifies!"

Much applause and cheering.

"Another approach, more specific, defines a miracle as an unexpected and unusual event which serves as a basis for credibility by showing the power of Christ and causes the witness to believe in Him! Now that is more like what I see! Miracles are more common than most realize and are not out of date as some would have us believe. I just don't believe in that oxymoron, minor miracle. Just ask someone who has had medically unexplained remissions of a previously diagnosed terminal disease just how minor it is! Any number of times, other small things for no apparent reason, a change of plans, direction, time, means of conveyance and such have resulted in the avoidance of tragedy. Luck? We know better! All of this is just a part of God's plan for us—His plan, not ours. It is not our place to categorize them nor do we need to know 'how He does that or why! Our only role is to continually acknowledge that He is with us, for us and deserving of our love and adoration.

A word of caution here—the dark side does miracles also! You can tell the difference though. Theirs only glorify man. The only real ones always, always glorify God.

Now to me, it's obvious that He was illustrating with Kurt in that fighter cockpit that we can choose Him and live or continue to do things our way and die. Same with Linda and Rick. When we lean on our own abilities and reasoning alone, not only are we doomed to crash, literally and figuratively, we, as examples may take those who depend on us down as well. Only with Him are all things truly possible!

So, we have established Who the architect is for this event and, I believe, defined the purpose for it as putting us on notice one more time that He hasn't gone away so we are still accountable. Anybody here besides me feel like Ezekiel's watchmen?"

Nervous laughter.

"You all know that I've been around about as long as dirt and I've been blessed to see some wonders our Lord has accomplished for, through and in spite of us. Let me tell you though that I thank Him especially for letting me not just see but be a part of what amounts to getting this Air Ministry off the ground! Pun intended!"

Groans and laughter.

"Think about all you have just heard and seen. The way the crew was brought together, Mrs. Johnssen's involvement with Rick and Linda, the fog delay, the crew illness, the flying of Gypsy, Kurt's miracle in itself, his conversion and work for the Lord—I'm not even going to get into that time thing!"

More cheers and laughter.

"It's all more than an old country preacher can absorb, but again, I thank God for letting me in on it. We are truly blessed to be here tonight and share in this moment. The Lord is truly here among us— feel it—open your hearts and clean out those dusty cobwebbed corners and let His Eternal Life giving light shine in and through you!"

Looking directly at Kelroy he proceeded,

"God does not waste miracles! There is always a purpose and, I repeat for effect, He always has the detailed plan. Nothing we have witnessed here was accidental. That includes the attendance of each of us. This is a time for priority checks of our lives".

"There is a lot of talk about the end times and 2012 and there may be something to some of it and I know that we are told that we won't know the time, but we are also told by Jesus that we need to pay attention to the signs around us. Now, if you are realistic about it, we shouldn't need to know the end time. Even if we had it confirmed that this world would be called to an end on December 21, 2012, what would that matter if your particular world ends tonight? Since we do not know, we should live every day as if it will be our last—it may well be! A delay in your decision to give your life to Christ could be a mistake with eternal consequences. Once you die outside of His Care, there will be no more chances. That is all there is to that!"

'If for any reason you still have doubts about the Creation and our Lord God Almighty, the Creator, I simply ask you to recall what you have just witnesses. If you have any plausible explanation for it, I ask you to please come down here right now and enlighten us all!"

More cheering and praising God.

At that, Kelroy and his aides got up and left the building amid shouts and applause. Graham Williams held up his hands,

"Prayer brothers and sisters, for touching and healing cold hearts. While we pray, each of us needs to ask for renewal in our lives that we may all go from here with a charge of the Holy Spirit straining within our hearts to be unleashed in this enemy world and that His Glory shine through each of us by our actions as 'doers of the Word'. Know this my family in Christ, the inspiration you need to feel will not come from Graham Williams. I'm not going to invite you to come down here to give your life to the Lord or to re-dedicate yourselves. I want you to fully understand that it's not important in the least that I or anybody in this building know or approve of your actions. That is between you and the Holy God who alone has the promise of salvation. Don't deceive yourselves by coming down here, supposedly full of the Spirit, then next week or sooner find yourselves like the seed sowed on shallow soil and have that zeal wither away. Unfortunately, that is common at these meetings. I and all the others that make up the Body of Christ are most anxious to welcome you, but there is nothing any of us can do until you first ask, not with your mouth, but with your heart that the Lord take over completely and guide you as His Own. Don't expect to hear from Him until you are sincerely repentant of your lost life and ask Him to show you how to change. That is when you truly present yourselves as a living sacrifice to Him."

There was a commotion in the back of the hangar. Everyone was stunned to silence as his two aides let the old nemesis, Kelroy, down the aisle to Graham.

"What happened? Are you alright? What is it, man?"

RICHARD COOK

After an awkward few moments of gathering himself, Kelroy asked to be directed to a microphone.

"Dr. Williams, ladies and gentlemen of the Air Ministry, members of the audience, please hear me."

Turning aside, weakly he said,

"I'm near shock so I should sit."

He was immediately seated and asked if he should be taken to the hospital.

"No, No, thank you, I'm okay, just a bit shaken and I MUST do this!"

After a few moments of gathering himself he continued,

"When I left here, I was somewhat confused as to what to make of the presentation, what I had seen, heard and, yes, felt. However, I fought through as my previous training had taught and was determined to use my experience here as an example of what effect the power of your fraudulent gimmicks could have on anyone, even one as immune to that foolishness as I am—or was. For that reason alone, I felt it my duty to do what I could to put an end to this before it did more harm, especially seeing the effect on all these people,"

Much grumbling, shouts and boos.

"Please, please, hear me out. I must tell you this! We got outside and my full former resolve returned. We began to discuss the plan of action to shut this down. At once, a bright column of light surrounded only me and I fell to the ground. A voice which seemed to come from all around me said, 'Ignatius, Ignatius, why are you persecuting me?' I asked who he was and he answered, 'I am the Lord, your God whom you are persecuting!'"

A wave of murmuring went throughout the crowd.

"I asked, 'Sir what do you want?' He answered, 'Ignatius, you are to get up and go back into the building where my people will help you. You are to relate these happenings and they will instruct you from there.' When I got up the light was gone. I stood there for a minute trying to regain my senses then I realized I was totally blind, as I still am."

Another roll of exclamations went through the crowd.

"My aides saw the light and heard the voice, so they were most eager to comply and get me back in here, so here we are!"

"The voice called you 'Ignatius'. Our records on you show that your middle name is Ivan."

"That is just one of many things that I am trying to process right now. Nobody on this earth could have known that the name I was born with was George Ignatius Kelroy. My father was the midwife when I was born and we lived in an area of few records and fewer inquiries, so there was never an official birth certificate generated for me at that time. My parents were killed in a house fire when I was five, we had no other family and the only surviving record listed me as George I. Kelroy. I hated that name even at that early age, so when I was placed in the orphanage, I told them the 'I' was for Ivan. It grew into legality with me, therefore, I repeat that no one could know that naturally!" After a long pause,

"Well, I was instructed to come in and relate to you what happened and then you would tell me what to do next. For once in my life, I am extremely attentive to anything you wish to tell me about this God—of ours!"

Anyone who was still seated jumped to their feet and all applauded and shouted praises to God. This would be a time that none present or watching the TV broadcast would ever forget. When the applause subsided, Graham said,

"Praise God yet again!"

More cheering as Kelroy spoke again,

"We were told about God in the orphanage school and I made a feeble attempt at prayer, but saw no change in my life, so I gave it up and eventually gave up on even the existence of God, much less Him hearing or caring about my life. I then decided that I was the only one I could count on and didn't need to have anybody including God. Well, I think He has my full attention now!"

"Mr. Kelroy, I can only tell you that, as surprised as you are and as we are, it is only one small example of the Mighty God we serve! As soon as we are able, we will all thank Him for His revelation to you. I must warn you sir, that He obviously has definite plans for you!"

More applause and cheering.

"We may have to re-name you one more time though, this time to Paul. I can hardly wait for you to read Acts 9."

Cheering and laughter.

"I ask now that we all as the one body we are, pray that the Lord free our brother George from his infirmity as he will now see with his heart and not his eyes only and can behold the glories this same merciful God has given us."

As the last amen faded, George literally leaped to his feet, went straight to the microphone and shouted,

"Lord, I thank you for your mercy on me, a worthless sinner. I don't know you yet but I will and so will everyone who comes into my range—praise to my God, I CAN SEE!"

The noise was incredible a everyone was out of their chairs and moving toward the now beaming George I. Kelroy, tears of joy streaming down his face.

Linda leaned to Rick,

"Guess we better order another uniform!"

"Yeah, I would say that folks are gonna know for sure that Kelroy was here!"